The

ESSENTIAL COLLECTION

#1 *New York Times* Bestselling Author

DEBBIE MACOMBER

FRIENDS—
and Then Some

D1324366

**HARLEQUIN**®
™ESSENTIAL DEBBIE MACOMBER COLLECTION

Recycling programs
for this product may
not exist in your area.

ISBN-13: 978-0-373-47305-2

FRIENDS—AND THEN SOME

For questions and comments about the quality of this book, please contact us at CustomerService@Harlequin.com.

Printed in U.S.A.

DEBBIE MACOMBER

is a number one *New York Times* and *USA TODAY* best-selling author. Her books include *1225 Christmas Tree Lane*, *1105 Yakima Street*, *A Turn in the Road*, *Hannah's List* and *Debbie Macomber's Christmas Cookbook*, as well as *Twenty Wishes*, *Summer on Blossom Street* and *Call Me Mrs. Miracle*. She has become a leading voice in women's fiction worldwide and her work has appeared on every major bestseller list, including those of the *New York Times*, *USA TODAY*, *Publishers Weekly* and *Entertainment Weekly*. She is a multiple award winner, and won the 2005 Quill Award for Best Romance. There are more than one hundred million copies of her books in print. Two of her Harlequin MIRA Christmas titles have been made into Hallmark Channel Original Movies, and the Hallmark Channel has launched a series based on her bestselling Cedar Cove series. For more information on Debbie and her books, visit her website, www.debbiemacomber.com.

One

The thick canvas sail flapped in the breeze before Jake Carson aligned the boat to catch the wind. The *Lucky Lady* responded by slicing through the choppy waters of San Francisco Bay. Satisfied, Jake leaned back and closed his eyes, content with his life and with the world.

"Do you think I'm being terribly mercenary?" Lily Morrissey asked as she stretched her legs out and crossed them at the ankles. "It sounds so coldhearted to decide to marry a man simply because he's wealthy. He doesn't have to be *that* rich." She paused to sigh expressively. Lately she'd given the matter consideration. For almost a year now she'd been playing the piano at the Wheaton. Only wealthy businessmen could afford to stay at a hotel as expensive as the Wheaton. And Lily was determined to find herself such a man. Unfortunately, no one had leaped forward, and she'd grown discouraged. Each day she told herself that she would meet someone soon. That hope was what kept Lily going back night after night.

"I'd only want someone rich enough to appreciate opera," she added thoughtfully. "Naturally it'd be nice if he drove a fancy car, but that isn't essential. All I really care about is his bank account. It's got to be large enough to take care of Gram and me. That doesn't sound so bad, does it?"

A faint smile tugged at the corners of Jake's mouth.

"Jake?" she repeated, slightly irritated.

"Hmm?"

"You haven't heard a word I said."

"Sure I have. You were talking about finding yourself a wealthy man."

"Yes, but that's what I always talk about. You could have guessed." Maybe she was foolish to dream of the day when a generous man would adorn her with diamonds.

"I wasn't guessing. I heard every word."

Lily studied him through narrowed eyes. "Sure you did," she mumbled under her breath.

Jake's slow, lazy smile came into play again.

Lily studied the profile of her best friend. Jake drove a taxi and they'd met the first week she worked at the Wheaton. She owed him a lot. Not only did he give her free rides back and forth to work when he was available, which was just about every day, but he'd rescued Gram and Lily from the Wheaton's manager.

Lily's starting salary had been less than what Gram had paid for an hour of piano lessons. Gram had raised Lily from the time her mother had died and her father had sought his fortune as a merchant marine. Gram had been outraged by the manager's unintended slight. And Gram, being Gram, couldn't do anything without a production. She'd shown up at the hotel in authentic witch doctor's costume and proceeded to chant a voodoo rite of retribution over the manager's head.

Luckily, Lily had gotten her grandmother out of the lobby before the police arrived. Jake had been standing next to his taxi and had witnessed the entire scene. Before everything exploded in Lily's face, Jake held open the cab door and whisked Gram and Lily away from any unpleasantness. Over the months that followed, the three had become good friends.

Jake was actually a struggling writer. He lived on his boat and worked hard enough to meet expenses by driving the taxi. He didn't seem to take anything too seriously. Not even his writing. Lily sometimes wondered how many other people he gave free rides to. Money didn't matter to Jake. But it did to Lily.

"I *am* going to meet someone," Lily continued on a serious note.

"I don't doubt it," Jake said and yawned, raising his hand to cover his mouth.

"I mean it, Jake. Tonight. I bet I meet someone tonight."

"For your sake, I hope you're right," Jake mumbled in reply.

Her words echoed in her ears several hours later when Lily pulled out the bench of the huge grand piano that dominated the central courtyard of the Wheaton. Dressed in her full-length sleeveless dress and dainty slippers, she was barely recognizable as the woman who'd spent the afternoon aboard Jake's boat.

Deftly her fingers moved over the smooth ivory keys as her upper body swayed with the melody of a Carpenters' hit.

Some days Lily felt that her smile was as artificial as her thick, curling eyelashes. After twenty-seven hundred times of hearing "Moon River," "Misty" and "Sentimental Journey," Lily was ready to take a journey herself. Maybe that was why she had talked to Jake. If she was going to meet someone, surely it would have happened by now. Sighing inwardly, she continued playing, hardly conscious of her fingers.

Five minutes later when Lily glanced up, she was surprised to find a ruddy faced cowboy standing next to the piano, watching her.

She smiled up at him and asked, "Is there something you'd like to hear?" He had to be close to forty-five, with the beginnings of a double chin. A huge turquoise buckle dominated the slight thickening at his waist. He was a good-looking man who was already going to seed.

"Do you know 'Santa Fe Gal of Mine'?" The slight Southern drawl wasn't a surprise. His head was topped with a Stetson although he was dressed in a linen sport coat that hadn't cost a penny under five hundred dollars. A Texan, she mused; a rich Texan, probably into oil.

"'Santa Fe Gal of Mine,'" she repeated aloud. "I'm not sure that I do," she answered with a warm smile. "Hum a few bars for me." She didn't usually get requests. People were more interested in checking into the hotel or meeting their friends for a drink in the sunken cocktail lounge to care about what she was playing.

The man placed a steadying hand against the side of the piano and momentarily closed his eyes. "I can't remember the melody," he admitted sheepishly. "Sorry, I'm not much good with that sort of thing. I'm an oilman not a singer."

So he was into oil just as she suspected. Lily got a glance at his feet and recognized the shoes from an advertisement she'd seen in *Gentlemen's Quarterly*. Cowboy boots, naturally, but ones made of imported leather and inlaid with silver. Leather, Lily felt, made the difference between being dressed and well dressed. This gentleman was definitely well dressed.

"Do you know who sang the popular version?" she questioned brightly, her heart pounding so hard it felt as though it would slam right out of her chest. She'd told Jake she was going to meet someone. And that someone had appeared at last! And he wasn't wearing a wedding band either.

"Nope, I can't say that I do."

"Maybe there's another song you'd like to hear?" Without conscious thought her hands continued to play as she glanced up at the cowboy with two chins and reminded herself that looks weren't everything. But, then again, maybe he had been married and had a son her age—an heir.

"One day I'm going to find some sweet gal who knows that blasted song," he muttered. "It always was my favorite."

Already Lily's mind had shifted into overdrive. Somehow she'd locate his long-lost song and gain his everlasting gratitude. "Will you be around tomorrow?"

"I should be."

"Come back and I'll see what I can do."

He straightened and gave her a brief salute. "I'll do that, little filly."

Lily's heart was pounding so hard that by the time she finished an hour later, she felt as if she'd been doing calisthenics. Maybe he'd be so grateful he'd insist on taking her to dinner. This could be the break Lily had waited months for. It hadn't happened exactly as she'd expected, but it was just the chance she'd been wanting. Already she could picture herself sitting in an elegant restaurant, ordering almond-saffron soup and lobster in wine sauce. For dessert she'd have Italian ice cream with walnuts and caramel oozing from the sides. Her mouth watered just thinking about all the wonderful foods she'd read about but never tasted. Her Texan would probably order barbecued chicken, but she wouldn't care. He could well be her ticket to riches and a genteel life…if she played her cards right. And for the first time in a long while, Lily felt she'd been dealt a hand of aces.

Jake was in his cab, parked in front of the hotel when she stepped into the balmy summer night. Eagerly she waved and hurried across the wide circular driveway to the bright-yellow taxi.

"Jake!" she cried. "Didn't I tell you today was the day? Didn't I? The most fantastically wonderful thing has happened! I can't believe I'm so lucky." She felt like holding out her arms and twirling around and bursting into song.

With one elbow leaning against the open window, Jake studied her with serious dark eyes and a slow, measured smile that lifted one corner of his full mouth. "Obviously Daddy Warbucks introduced himself."

"Yes," she giggled. "*My* Daddy Warbucks."

Leaning across the front seat, Jake swung open the passenger door. "Climb in and you can tell me all about it on the way to your house."

Rushing around the front of the car, Lily scooted inside the cab and closed the door. Jake started the engine and pulled onto the busy street, skillfully merging with the flowing traffic. "I was so surprised, I nearly missed my chance," Lily started up again. "Suddenly, after all these months, he was there in a five-hundred-dollar sport coat, requesting a song. He called me 'little filly,' and, Jake, he's rich. Really, really rich. I can just see that Texas oil oozing from every pore." She paused long enough to inhale before continuing. "He's older, maybe forty-five or fifty, but that's not so bad. And he's nice. I can tell that about a man. Remember how I met you and instantly knew what a great person you were? That's just the kind of feeling I had tonight." She continued chattering for another full minute until she realized how quiet Jake had become. "Oh, Jake, I'm sorry, I've been talking up a storm without giving you a chance to think."

"You're talking with a drawl."

"Oh, yeah, I'm practicing. I was born in Texas, you know."

"You were?"

"No, of course not, but I thought it'd impress him."

The slow, lazy smile came into play again.

Lily studied the intense profile of her friend as he steered. Jake wasn't handsome—not in the way the models for *Gentlemen's Quarterly* were. He was tall with broad shoulders and a muscular build. But with those sea-green eyes and that dark hair, he could be attractive if he tried. Only Jake couldn't care less. Half the time he dressed in faded jeans and outdated sweaters. Lily doubted that he even owned a suit. Formal wear wasn't part of Jake's image.

As she studied Jake, Lily realized that she really didn't know much about him. Jake kept the past to himself. She knew he'd been a medic in the Army, and had an engineering degree from a prestigious college back east someplace. From tidbits of conversation here and there, she'd learned that he'd worked at every type of job imaginable. There didn't seem to be anything he hadn't tried once and— if he liked it—done again and again. In some ways Jake reminded Lily of her father who had been in the merchant marine and brought her a storehouse of treasures from around the world. Jake was the kind of man who could do anything he put his mind to. He was creative and intelligent, proud and resourceful.

Lily supposed she loved him but only as a friend. He was her confidant and in many ways, her partner. Her feelings were more like those of a young girl for an endearing older brother or an adventurous sidekick. Love, real love between a man and a woman was an emotion Lily held in reserve for her husband. But first she had to convince a rich man that she would be an excellent wife.

Studying Jake now, Lily noted that something had displeased him. She could tell by the way he tucked back his chin, giving an imitation of a cobra prepared to strike. He exuded impatience and restrained anger. From past experience, Lily knew that whatever was bothering him would be divulged in his own time and in his own way.

"Well?" he snapped.

"Well, what?"

"Are you going to tell me your plan to snag this rich guy or not?"

"Are you sure you want to hear? You sound like you want to snap my head off."

"Darn it, Lily, one of these days..." He paused to inhale sharply as if the night were responsible for his wrath. Several moments passed before he spoke, and when he did his voice was as smooth as velvet, almost caressing.

Lily wasn't fooled. Jake was furious. "All right, tell me what's wrong. Did you get stiffed again? I thought you had a foolproof system for avoiding that."

"No one stiffed me."

"Then what?"

He ignored her, seeming to concentrate on the traffic. "Listen, kid, you've got to be careful."

Lily hated it when Jake called her "kid" and he knew it. "Be careful? What are you talking about? You're acting like I'm planning to handle toxic waste. Good grief, I don't even know his name."

"You could be playing with fire."

"I'm not playing anything yet. Which reminds me, have you ever heard the song 'Santa Fe Gal of Mine'?"

"'Santa Fe Gal of Mine'?" The harsh disgruntled look left his expression as a smile split his mouth. "No, I can't say that I have."

"Gram will know it," Lily said with complete confidence. Her grandmother might be a bit eccentric, but the woman was a virtual warehouse of useless information. If that wealthy Texan's favorite song was ever on the charts, Gram would know it.

Jake eased to a stop in front of the large two-story house with the wide front porch.

"Can you come in now or will you be by later?"

"Later," he answered with apparent indifference.

Lily walked toward the house and

paused on the front steps, confused again. A disturbing shiver trembled through her at the cool, appraising way Jake had behaved this evening. His smooth, impenetrable green eyes resembled the dark jade Buddha her father had brought her from Hong Kong. Nothing about Jake had been the same tonight. Lily attributed it to his having had a bad day. But it shouldn't have been. They'd spent the majority of it sailing and they both loved that. But then everyone had a bad day now and again. Jake was entitled to his.

Shaking off the feelings of unease, Lily stepped inside the fifty-year-old house, pausing to pat Herbie. Herbie was her grandmother's favorite conversation piece—a shrunken head from South America. A zebra-skin rug from Africa rested in front of the fireplace.

The television blared from Gram's bedroom, but the older woman was snoring just as loudly, drowning out the sounds of the cops-and-robbers movie. With an affectionate smile, Lily turned off the set and quietly tiptoed from the darkened room. She'd talk to Gram in the morning.

After changing out of the red gown, Lily inspected her limited wardrobe, wondering what she'd wear first if the Texan asked her to dinner. Possibly the dress with the plunging neckline. No, she mentally argued with herself. That dress could give him the wrong impression. The lavender chiffon one she'd picked up at Repeaters, a second-hand store, looked good with her dark eyes and had a high neckline. Lily felt it would be best to start this relationship off right. She was sitting beside the old upright piano, sorting through Gram's sheet music that was stored in the bench when Jake returned. He let himself in, hung his jacket on the elephant tusks and picked up a discarded Glenn Miller piece from the top of the pile.

"Hi."

"Hi." At least he sounded in a better mood than earlier. "It'd be just like Gram to have that song and not even know it."

"You're determined to find it, aren't you?" Jake asked with a faint smile.

"I've got to find it," Lily shot back. "Everything will be ruined if I don't." Her sharp words bounced back without penetrating his aloof composure. "He won't be grateful if I can't find that song."

Jake sat on the arm of the sofa and idly flipped through the stack she'd already sorted. He didn't like the sounds of this Texan. He wasn't sure what he was feeling. Lily was determined to find herself a rich man and, knowing her persistence, Jake thought she probably would. When Lily wanted something, she went after it with unwavering resolve. In his life, there wasn't anything he cared that much about. Sure, there were things he wanted, but nothing that was worth abandoning the easygoing existence he had now. Lily's dark-brown eyes had sparkled with eager excitement when she'd told him about the Texan. He'd never seen anyone's eyes light up that way.

"Did you get a chance to do any writing today?"

Jake straightened the tall stack of sheet music and sat upright. "I finished that short story I was telling you about and e-mailed it off."

Lily smiled up at him, her attention diverted for the moment. Jake had talent, but he wasted it on short stories that didn't sell when he should be concentrating on a novel. That's where the real money was. "Are you going to let me read this one?" He usually gave her his work to look over, mainly for grammar and spelling errors—Jake was a "creative" speller.

"Later," he hedged, not knowing why. He preferred it when Lily had a chance to correct his blatant errors, but there was something of himself in this story that he'd held in reserve, not wishing her to see. The interesting part of being a writer was that Jake didn't always like the people inside him who appeared on paper. Some were light and witty while others were dark and dangerous. None were like him and yet each one was a part of himself.

"I know Gram's got tons more sheet music than this," Lily mumbled, thoughtfully chewing on her bottom lip. "Do you want to go to the attic with me?"

"Sure."

He followed her up the creaky stairs to the second floor, then moved in front and opened the door that led to another staircase, this one narrower and steeper. Lily tucked her index finger in Jake's belt loop as the light from the hallway dimmed. They were surrounded by the pitch-black dark, two steps into the attic.

"Where's the light?"

An eerie sensation slowly crept up Lily's arm and settled in her stomach. The air was still with a stagnant heaviness. "In the center someplace. Jake, I'll do this tomorrow. It's creepy up here."

"We're here now," he argued and half turned, bringing her to his side and loosely taking her by the hand. "Don't worry, I'll protect you."

"Yeah, that's what I'm afraid of." She tried to make light of her apprehensions, and managed to squelch the urge to turn back toward the dim hallway light. Involuntarily she shivered. "Gram's got some weird stuff up here."

"It can't be any worse than what's downstairs," he murmured, and chuckled softly as he edged their way into the black void, taking short steps as he swung his hand out in front of him to prevent a collision with some inanimate object.

Gradually, Lily's eyes adjusted to the lack of light. "I think I see the string—to your left there." She pointed for his benefit and squeezed her eyes half-closed for a better view. It didn't look exactly right, but it could be the light.

"That's a hangman's noose."

"Good grief, what's Gram doing with that?" In some ways, she'd rather not know what treasures Gram had stored up here. The attic was Gram's territory and Lily hadn't paid it a visit in years. In truth, Lily didn't really want to know what her sweet grandmother was doing with a hangman's noose.

"She told me once that her great-grandfather is said to have ridden with Jesse James. The noose might have something to do with that." As he spoke, Jake's foot collided with a box and he stumbled forward a few steps until he regained his balance.

Lily let out a sharp gasp, then held her breath. "Are you all right?"

"I'm fine."

"What was that?"

"How would I know?"

"Jake, let's go back down. Please." Her greatest fear was walking into a bat's nest or something worse.

"We already went over that. The light's got to be around here someplace."

"Sure, and in the meantime we don't know..."

"Damn."

Lily's hand tightened around his, her fingers clammy. "Now what's wrong?"

"My knee bumped into something."

"That does it. We're going back." Jake could stay up here if he wanted, but she was leaving. From the minute they'd stepped inside this tomb, Lily had felt uneasy.

"Lily," he argued.

Jerking her hand free, she turned toward the stairs and the faint beam of light. It looked as though the attic door had eased shut, cutting off what little illumination there had been from the hall. Everything was terribly dark and spooky. "I'm getting out of here," she declared, unable to keep the catch out of her voice. "This place is giving me the heebie-jeebies." More interested in making her escape than being cautious, Lily turned away and walked straight into a spider's web. A disgusted sound slid from her throat as her hands flew up to free her face from the fine, sticky threads. A prickling fear shot up her spine as she felt something scamper across her foot.

Her heart rammed against her breast like a jackhammer as the terror gripped her and she let out a bloodcurdling cry. "Jake…Jake."

He was with her in seconds, roughly pulling her into his arms. She clung to him, frantically wrapping her arms around his neck. Her face was buried in his shoulder as she trembled. His arms around her waist half lifted her from the floor. "Lily, you're all right," he whispered frantically. His hold, secure and warm, drove out the terror. "I've got you." It took all the strength she could muster just to nod.

Jake's hand brushed the wispy curls from her temple. "Lily," he repeated soothingly. "I told you I'd protect you." His warm breath fanned her face, creating an entirely new set of sensations. His scent, a combination of sweat and man, was unbelievably intoxicating. For the first time Lily became aware of how tightly pressed her body was to the rock hardness of his. Her grip slackened and she slid intimately down the length of him until her feet touched the floor. The hem of her blouse rode up, exposing her midriff so that her bare skin rubbed against the muscular wall of his chest. His hands found their place in the small of her back and seemed to hold her there, pressing her all the closer. Her breasts were flattened to his upper torso and her nerves fired to life at the merest brush of his body.

As if hypnotized, their eyes met and held in the faint light. It was as though they were seeing each other for the first time. Her pulse fluttered wildly at his look of curious surprise as his gaze lowered to her mouth.

"Jake?" Her voice was the faintest whisper, wavering and unsure.

His eyes darkened and a thick frown formed on his face. Slowly, almost as if drawn by something other than his will, Jake lowered his mouth to hers. Warm lips met warm lips in an exploratory kiss that was as gentle as it was unhurried. "Lily." His mouth left hers and sounded oddly raspy and unsure. Her eyes remained tightly closed.

Somehow she found her voice. "That shouldn't have happened."

"Do you want an apology?"

Her arms slid from around his neck and fell to her side as he released her. "No..." she whispered. "I should be the one to apologize...I don't know what came over me."

"You're right about this place," he admitted on a harsh note. "There is something spooky about it. Let's get out of here."

By the time they'd returned to the living room, Lily had regained her equilibrium and could smile over the peculiar events in the attic.

"What's so amusing?" He didn't sound the least bit pleased by their adventure, and stalked ahead of her, sitting in the fan-back bamboo chair usually reserved for Gram.

"Honestly, Jake, can you imagine *us kissing*?"

"We just did," he reminded her soberly, his voice firm as his watchful eyes studied her. "And if we're both smart, we'll forget it ever happened."

Lily sat on the sofa, tucking her legs under her. "I suppose you're right. It's just that after being such good friends for the past year, it was a shock. Elaine would never forgive me."

"Would you lay off Elaine? I've told you a thousand times that it's been over for months." Jake grimaced at the sound of the other woman's name. His relationship with Elaine Wittenberg had developed nicely in the beginning. She was impressed with his writing, encouraging even. Then bit by bit, with intrusive politeness, Elaine had started to reorganize his life. First came the suggestion that he change jobs. Driving a cab didn't pay that well, and with his talents he could do anything. She started introducing him to her friends, making contacts for him. The problem was that Jake liked his life exactly the way it was. Elaine had been a close call—too close. Jake had come within inches of waking up one morning living in a three-bedroom house with a white picket fence and a new car parked in the garage—a house and a car with big monthly payments. True, Lily was just as eager for the same material possessions, but at least she was honest about it.

"Well, you needn't worry," Lily told him, taking a deep breath and releasing it slowly. "Just because we kissed, it doesn't mean anything."

Her logic irritated him. "Let's not talk about it, all right? It was a mistake and it's over."

Lily arched a delicate brow and

shrugged one shoulder. "Fine." His attitude didn't please her in the least. As far as she knew, Jake wasn't one to sweep things under the carpet and forget they existed. If anything, he faced life head-on.

Abruptly getting to his feet, Jake stalked to the other side of the living room. Confused, Lily watched the impatient, angry way he moved. "I'll see you tomorrow," he said on his way to the front door.

"Okay."

The door closed and Lily didn't move. What an incredibly strange night it had been. First, the golden opportunity of finding that crazy song for the Texan. Then, wilder still was Jake's kissing her in the attic. Even now she could feel the pressure of his mouth on hers, and the salty-sweet taste of him lingered on her lips. He'd held her close, his scent heightened by the stuffy air of the attic.

But, Lily realized with a start, the kiss had been a moment out of time and was never meant to be. Jake was right. They should simply put it out of their minds and forget it had happened. A single kiss should be no threat to a year of solid friendship. They knew each other too well to get caught up in a romantic relationship. Lily had seen the type of woman Jake usually went for, and she wasn't even close to it. Jake's ideal woman was Mother Theresa, Angelina Jolie and Betty Crocker all rolled into one perfect female specimen. Conversely, her ideal man was Daddy Warbucks, Bruce Willis and Mr. Goodwrench. No…Jake and she would always be friends; they'd make terrible lovers….

The next morning when Lily found her way into the kitchen, Gram was already up and about. Her bright-red hair was tightly curled into a hundred ringlets and held in place with bobby pins.

"Morning," Lily mumbled and pulled out a kitchen chair, eager to speak to her grandmother.

Gram didn't acknowledge the greeting. Instead, the older woman concentrated on opening a variety of bottles, extracting her daily quota of pills.

Lily waited until her grandmother had finished swallowing thirteen garlic tablets and a number of vitamins, and had chewed six blanched almonds. This daily ritual was Gram's protection from cancer. The world could scoff, but at seventy-four Gram was as fit as someone twenty years her junior.

"I didn't hear you come in last night."

A smile played at the edges of Lily's mouth. "I know. Gram, have you ever heard of the song 'Santa Fe Gal of Mine'?"

The older woman's look was thoughtful and Lily nibbled nervously on her bottom lip. "It's been a lotta years since I heard that ol' song."

"You remember it?" Relief washed through Lily until she sagged against the back of the chair. Lily marveled again at her grandmother's memory.

"Play a few bars for me, girl."

Lily tensed and the silence stretched until her nerve endings screamed with it. "I don't know the song, Gram. I thought *you* did."

"I do," she insisted, shaking her bright red head. "I don't remember it offhand, is all."

Is all, Lily repeated mentally in a panic. "When do you think you'll remember it?"

"I can't rightly say. Give me a day or two."

A day or two! "Gram, I haven't got that long. Our future could depend on 'Santa Fe Gal of Mine.' Think."

Stirring the peanut butter with a knife, Gram picked up a soda cracker and dabbed a layer of chunky-style spread across the top before popping it into her mouth.

Lily wanted to scream that this wasn't a time for food, but she pressed her lips tightly shut, forcing down the panic. Gram didn't do well under pressure.

"What do you want to know for?" Gram asked after a good five minutes had lapsed. Meanwhile, she'd eaten six soda crackers, each loaded with a thick layer of peanut butter.

"A rich man requested that song last night. A very rich man who had a generous look about him," Lily explained, doing her best to keep the excitement out of her voice. "If I can come up with that song, he'd probably be willing to show his appreciation."

"We could use a little appreciation, couldn't we, girl?"

"Oh, Gram, you know we could."

"If I can't think of it, Gene Autry would know." Gram often spoke as if famous personalities were her lifelong friends and all she had to do was pick up the phone and give a jingle.

"Did Gene Autry sing the original version?"

"Now that you mention it, he might have been the one," she said, scratching the side of her head.

Lily perked up. Gram had a recording of every song Gene Autry had ever sung. "Then you have it."

"I must," she agreed. "Someplace."

"Someplace" turned out to be in the furnace room in the basement five hours later. The next few hours were spent transposing the scratchy old record into notes Lily could play on the piano.

When she sat at the grand piano at five that evening in the Wheaton lobby, 'Santa Fe Gal of Mine' was forever embedded in her brain. Each note had been agonized over. There couldn't be a worse way to memorize a song. Lily had never been able to play very well by ear.

As it worked out, the timing had been tight and consequently Lily had been unable to pay the amount of attention she would have liked to her dress and makeup.

The lobby was busy with people strolling in and out, registering for a wholesale managers' conference. At the moment the only thing Lily was interested in was one Texan with a love for an ol' Gene Autry number.

During the evening, Lily twice played the song she had come to hate more than any of the others. Her only reward was a few disgruntled stares. The lively Western piece wasn't the "elevator" style she'd been hired to play. The second go-around with 'Santa Fe Gal' and Lily caught the manager's disapproving stare.

Instantly, Lily switched over to something he'd consider more appropriate: 'Moon River.'

As the evening progressed, Lily's plastic smile became more and more forced. She'd gone to all this trouble for nothing. Her stomach felt as if it were weighted with a lead balloon. All the hassle she'd gone through, all the work, had been for nothing. Gram would be so disappointed. Heavens, Gram nothing. Lily felt like crying.

As usual, Jake was waiting for her outside the hotel.

"How'd it go?" he asked as she approached the cab. One look at her sorrowful dark eyes and Jake climbed out of the cab. "What happened?"

"Nothing."

"Mr. Moneybags wasn't the appreciative type?"

She shook her head, half expecting

Jake to scold her for being so incredibly naive. "No."

"What, then?"

"He didn't show."

Jake held open the taxi door for her. "Oh, Lily, I'm sorry."

"It's not your fault," she returned loyally. "I was the stupid one. I can't believe that I could have gotten so excited over an overweight Texan who wanted to hear a crummy song that's older than I am."

"But he was a rich Texan."

"Into oil and maybe even gold."

"Maybe," Jake repeated.

He'd walked around the front of the taxi when the captain of the bellboys came hurrying out of the hotel. "Miss Lily!" he called, flagging her down. "Someone left a message for you."

Two

"A message?" Lily's gaze clashed with Jake's as excitement welled up inside her, lifting the dark shroud of depression that had settled over her earlier.

"Thanks, Henry." Lily gave the hotel's senior bellhop a brilliant smile. Two minutes before, Lily would never have believed that something as simple as an envelope could chase the clouds of doubt from her heart.

"Well, what does it say?" Jake questioned, leaning through the open car window. He appeared as anxious as Lily.

"Give me a minute to open it, for heav-

en's sake." She ripped apart the beige envelope bearing the Wheaton's logo. Her
gaze flew over the bold pen-strokes,
reading as fast as she could. "It's him."

"Daddy Warbucks?"

"Yes," she repeated, her voice qua-
vering with anticipation. "Only his real
name is Rex Flanders. He says he got
hung up in a meeting and couldn't make
it downstairs, but he wanted me to know
he heard the song and it was just as good
as he remembered. He wants to thank
me." Searching for something more, Lily
turned over the single sheet, thinking
she must have missed or dropped it in
her hastiness. Surely he meant that he
wanted to thank her with more than a
simple message. The least she'd expected
was a dinner invitation. With hurried,
anxious movements she checked her lap,
scrambling to locate the envelope she'd

so carelessly discarded only a moment before.

"What are you looking for?" Jake asked, perplexed.

"Nothing." Defeat caused her voice to drop half an octave. Lily couldn't take her eyes from the few scribbled lines on the single sheet of hotel stationery. Shaking her head, she hoped to clear her muddled thoughts. She'd been stupid to expect anything more than a simple thank-you. Rich men always had women chasing after them. There wasn't one thing that would make her stand out in a crowd. She wasn't strikingly beautiful, or talented, or even sophisticated. Little about her would make her attractive to a wealthy man.

"Lily?" Gently, Jake placed a hand on her forearm. His tender touch warmed her cool skin and brought feeling back to her numb fingers. "What's wrong?"

A tremulous smile briefly touched her lips. "Me. I'm wrong. Oh, Jake, I'm never going to find a rich man who'll want to marry me. And even if I caught someone's eye, they'd take one look at Gram and Herbie and start running in the opposite direction."

"I don't see why," he contradicted sharply. "I didn't."

"Yeah, but you're just as weird as we are."

"Thanks." Sarcasm coated his tongue. So Lily thought he was as eccentric as her grandmother. All right, he'd agree that he didn't show the corporate ambitions that drove so many of his college friends. He liked his life. He was perfectly content to live on a sailboat for the remainder of his days, without a care or responsibility. There wasn't anything in this world that he couldn't walk away from, and that was exactly the way he wanted it. No complications. No one to answer to. Except Gram and Lily. But even now his platonic relationship with Lily was beginning to cause problems. He admired Lily. What he liked best about her was that she had no designs on his heart and no desire to change him. She was an honest, forthright woman. She knew what she wanted and made no bones about it. Their kiss from the day before had been a fluke that wouldn't happen again. He'd make sure of that.

"I didn't mean that the way it sounded," Lily mumbled her apology. "You're the best friend I've got. I'm feeling a bit defeated at the moment. Tomorrow I'll be back to my normal self again."

Silently walking around the front of the taxi, Jake climbed into the driver's seat and started the engine with a flick of his wrist. "I can't say I blame you." And he didn't. After everything she'd gone through to find that song, she had every right to be disappointed.

"It's me I'm angry with," Lily said, breaking the silence. "I shouldn't have put such stock in a simple request."

Jake blamed himself. He should have cautioned her, but at the time he'd been so surprised that he hadn't known what he was feeling—maybe even a bit of jealousy, which had shocked the hell out of him. Later he'd discarded that notion. He wanted Lily to be as happy as she deserved, but there was something about this Texan that had troubled him from the beginning.

The moment Lily had mentioned she'd met someone, warning lights had gone off inside his head. His protective instinct, for some reason he couldn't put into words, had been aroused. That alien impulse had been the cause of the incident in the attic. He didn't regret kissing Lily, but it was just that type of thing that could ruin a good friendship. The Texan meant trouble for Lily. It'd taken him half the night to realize that was what bothered him, but he was certain. Now, after Lily's revelation, Jake could afford to be generous.

"How about if we go fishing tomorrow?"

Lily straightened, her dark eyes glowing with pleasure at the invitation. Over the past year, Jake had only taken her out on the sloop for short, limited periods of time. Lily loved sailing and was convinced that the man she married would have to own a sailboat.

"With Gram," he added, smiling. "We'll make a day of it, pack a bottle of good wine, some cheese and a loaf of freshly baked French bread, and beer for me."

"Jake, that sounds wonderful." Al-

ready her heart was lifting with anticipation. Only Jake would know that an
entire day on his sailboat would cheer
her up like this.

"We deserve a one-day vacation from
life. I'll park the cab, shut down the laptop and take you to places you have
never been."

Lily expelled a deep sigh of content-
ment. "It sounds great, but Thursday's
Gram's bingo day. Nothing will convince her to give that up."

A smile sparked from Jake's cool jade
eyes. Lily's grandmother had her own
get-rich schemes going. "Then it'll have
to be the two of us. Are you still game?"

"You bet." Lily pictured the brisk wind
whipping her hair freely about her face
as the boat sliced through the deep-green
waters of San Francisco Bay.

Within ten hours, the daydream had
become reality. The wind carried Lily's
low laugh as she tossed back her head

and the warm breeze ruffled her thick, unbound hair. The boat keeled sharply and cut a deep path through the choppy water. Lily had climbed to the front of the boat to raise the sails and was now sitting on the bow, luxuriating in the overwhelming sense of freedom she was experiencing. She wanted to capture this utopian state of being and hug it to her breast forever. She didn't dare turn back and let Jake see her. He'd laugh at her childish spirit and tease her unmercifully. Lily wanted nothing to ruin the magnificent day.

For the first hour of their trip, Lily remained forward while Jake manned the helm. Keeping his mind to the task was difficult. He couldn't ever remember seeing Lily so carefree and happy. She was a natural sailor. He'd taken other women aboard *Lucky Lady* and always regretted it. Elaine, for one. In the beginning, she'd pretended to love his boat as much as he, but Jake hadn't been fooled. Elaine's big mistake had come when she suggested that he move off the boat and into an apartment. Pitted against his only true love, Jake decided to keep *Lady* and dump Elaine. And not a moment since had he regretted the decision.

Watching Lily produced a curious sense of pride in Jake. Laughing, she turned back and shouted something to him. The wind whirled her voice away and he hadn't a clue as to what she'd said, but the exhilaration in her flushed face wasn't something that could be manufactured. It surprised Jake how much he enjoyed watching her. She reminded him of the sea nymphs sailors of old claimed inhabited the waters.

As he watched her, Jake realized that Lily was his friend and they were fortunate to share a special kind of relationship. But it wasn't until that moment that Jake noticed just how beautiful she was. In the year he'd known her, Lily's youthful features had filled out with vivid promise. Her long hair was a rich, dark shade of mahogany and he'd rarely seen it unbound. That day, instead of piling it on top of her head the way she normally did, Lily had left it free so that it fell in gentle waves around her shoulders. Her natural gracefulness was what struck Jake most. Her walk was decidedly provocative. Jake smiled to himself with an inner pride at the interest Lily's gently rounded hips generated from the opposite sex. If that Texan had seen her walk he would have given her more than a simple thank you. But what Jake loved mainly about Lily was her eyes. Never in his life had he met anyone with eyes so dark and expressive. Some days they were like cellophane and he could read her moods as clearly as the words in a book. He could imagine what it would be like making love to her. He wouldn't need to see anything but her eyes to...

He shook his head and dispelled the disconcerting thoughts. His fingers tightened around the helm and he looked sharply out to sea.What was the matter with him? He was thinking of Lily as a prospective lover.

"How about a cup of coffee?" Lily called, standing beside the mast. The wind whipped her hair behind her like a magnificent flag and Jake sucked in his breath at the sight of her.

"I'll get it," he shouted. "Take over here for me, will you?"

A quick, tantalizing smile spread across her features as she nodded and hurried down to join him at the helm. She laughed as he gave her careful instructions. She didn't need them. She felt giddy and reckless and wonderful.

Turning away, it was all Jake could do not to kiss her again. Mumbling under his breath, he descended to the galley and sleeping area of the boat.

Lily didn't know what was troubling Jake. She'd witnessed the dark scowl on his face and been surprised. He returned a few minutes later with two steaming mugs, handing her one.

"Is something wrong?" she ventured.

"Nothing," he said, keeping his gaze from lingering on her soft, inviting mouth.

"You look like you want to bite off my head again."

"Again?" Jake was stalling for time. This foul mood was Lily's fault. She didn't know what she was doing to him, and that was his problem.

"Yes, again," she repeated. "Like you did the other night when I told you about Rex."

"I've been doing some thinking about

that ungrateful Texan," he said, narrowing his eyes. "There's something about him I don't trust."

"But you've never seen him," Lily countered, confused.

"I didn't have to. Just hearing about him was enough. I don't want you to see him again."

"Jake!"

"I mean it, Lily."

Astonished, Lily sat with her jaw sagging and turned away from him, cupping the steaming mug with both hands. Jake had never asked her to do anything. It wasn't like him to suddenly order her about and make demands. She swallowed her indignation. "Will you give me a reason?"

Drawing in a deep, irritated breath, Jake looked out over the green water and wondered at his own high-handedness. The Texan had been bothering him for two days. He hadn't wanted to say anything and even now, he wasn't entirely convinced he was doing the right thing. "It's a gut feeling I have. My instincts got me out of the war alive. I can't explain it, Lily, but I'm asking you to trust me in this."

"All right," she agreed, somewhat deflated. At the rate things were progressing with Rex What's-his-name, she wouldn't have the opportunity to see him again anyway. In reality, Jake wasn't asking much. He was her friend and she trusted his judgment, albeit at the moment reluctantly.

"Someone else will come along," Jake assured her, and a lazy grin crept across his face. "If not, you'll trap one as effectively as the fish we're about to lure to our dinner plates."

"You make it sound too easy." He wasn't the one who sat at that piano night after night playing those same songs again and again and again.

"It is." He handed her a fishing pole and carefully revealed to her the finer points of casting. Luckily, Lily was a fast learner and he took pains not to touch her. Shaking off his mood, he gave her a friendly smile. "Before you know it, our meal will mosey along," he said with a distinct Southern drawl. "And who knows? It could be an oil-rich Texan bass."

Lily laughed, enjoying their light banter.

"Every woman scheming to marry money has to keep her eye out for a tightfisted shark, but then again—" he paused for emphasis "—you might stumble upon a flounder in commodities."

"A generous flounder," Lily added.

"Naturally." Cupping his hand behind his head, Jake leaned back, crossed his long legs at the ankle and closed his eyes. He felt better. He hadn't a clue why he felt so strongly about that rich Texan. He just sensed trouble.

"There's another message for you, Miss Lily," Henry informed her when she arrived at the hotel the following evening.

Lily stared at the envelope as if it were a snake about to lash out at her. "A message?" she repeated, her voice sounding like an echo.

"From the same man as before," Henry explained with ageless, questioning eyes.

Undoubtedly the elderly bellboy couldn't understand her reluctance now when only the day before she behaved as if she'd won the lottery.

"Thank you." Lily took the folded note and made her way into the grand lobby. The manager acknowledged her with a faint nod, but Lily's answering smile was forced. The message lay on the keyboard of the piano for several moments before she had the courage to open it.

> Hello, Lily—the bellhop told me your name. He also told me what time you'd be in today. I've thought about you and your music. I'm hoping that a sweet filly like you won't think it too forward of me to suggest we meet later for a drink.
>
> *Rex Flanders*

A drink…surely that would be harmless, especially if they stayed right here in the hotel. Jake wouldn't mind that. Her hands moved to the ivory keys and automatically began the repertoire of songs that was only a step above the canned music that played in elevators.

Although her fingers moved with practiced ease, Lily's thoughts were in turmoil. She'd promised Jake she wouldn't get involved with Rex. At the time it had seemed like a little thing. It hadn't seemed likely she'd have the chance to see him again. Now she regretted having consented to Jake's request so readily. Her big break had arrived and she was going to have to refuse probably the richest man she'd ever met. And all because Jake had some stupid *feeling*. It wasn't fair. How could anyone have a feeling about someone they hadn't even met?

Later, when she had a moment, Lily penned a note to Rex, declining his invitation. She didn't offer an excuse. It'd sound ludicrous to explain that a friend had warned her against him. *You see, my friend, Jake, who has never even met you, has decided you're bad news. He felt so strongly about it that he made me promise I wouldn't see you again.* Rex would laugh himself all the way home to Texas. No one in their right mind would blame him.

Jake was out front, standing beside his taxi when she appeared. She suddenly felt like taking the bus, but one look at the darkening sky convinced her otherwise. The night was overcast, with thick gray clouds rolling in over the bay. Lily didn't need the weather to dampen her already foul mood.

"I hope you're happy," she announced as she opened the car door.

"Relatively. What's your problem?"

"At the moment, you."

Their gazes met, a clash of befuddled emerald and blazing jet. Lily had been waiting months for this opportunity— months of built up fanciful dreams— months when she'd schemed and planned for exactly this moment. And now, because of Jake, she was walking away from the opportunity of a lifetime.

"Me!" Jake cocked his head to one side, studying her as his gaze narrowed thoughtfully. "What do you mean?" His tone told her clearly that he didn't appreciate being put on the defensive.

"Rex asked me out."

"And you refused?" Instinctively he felt the hard muscles of his shoulders tense. So Daddy Warbucks was back. Somehow Jake had known the man would return.

"I'm here, aren't I? But I'll have you know that I regret that promise and would take it back in a minute if you'd let me." She eyed him hopefully, but at the sight of the deep grooves that were forming at the sides of his mouth, Lily could tell he wouldn't relent.

Jake was conscious of an odd sensation surging through his blood. He'd experienced it only a few times in his life and always when something monumental was about to happen. The first time had been as an eight-year-old kid. He'd been lost in the downtown area at Christmastime and frightened half out of his wits. The huge skyscrapers had seemed to close in around him until he could taste panic. Then, the feeling had come and he'd stopped, got his bearings and found his way home on his own, astonishing his mother. Later, in high school, that same feeling had struck right before he played in a football game during which he scored three touchdowns and went on to be the MVP for the season. He'd felt it again in the desert in Iraq and that time, it had saved his life. Jake had never told anyone about the feeling. It was too complex to define.

"No," he said with cold deliberation. "I'm not changing my mind."

"Jake," she moaned, feeling wretched.

"I'm asking you to trust me." He said it without looking at her, not wanting her to see the intensity of his determination. His fists were clenched so tightly at his sides that his fingers ached. Lily could bat her long eyelashes at him all she wanted and it wouldn't change how he felt. Truth be known, he wished she'd find her Daddy Warbucks and get married if that was what she wanted so badly. But this Texan wasn't the right man for Lily.

Without further discussion, Lily slid inside the cab. Disappointment caused her shoulders to droop and her head to hang so low that her chin rested against the bright-red collar of her gown. She was more tired than she could remember having been in a long time. Of all the men in the world, she trusted Jake the most. More than her father. But then it was difficult to have too much confidence in a vague childhood memory. Lily's father had died when she was twelve, but she had trouble picturing him in her mind. As far as Lily could recall, she'd only seen her father a handful of times. In some ways Lily wished she didn't trust Jake so much; it would make things a whole lot easier.

Jake closed her door, his hands gripping the open window as he watched her through weary eyes. For half a second, he toyed with the idea of releasing her from the promise. But he entertained the idea only fleetingly. He knew better.

"Can you take me home now?"

"Sure." He hurried around the cab and climbed into the front seat beside her. A flick of the key and the engine purred. "You won't regret this," Jake said, flashing her one of his most brilliant smiles.

"I regret it already," she said and stared out the side window.

Those thoughtless words hounded Lily for the remainder of the evening. Jake was her friend—her best friend—and she was treating him like the tax man. Usually, at the end of the evening Jake would stop by the house on his way back to the dock where his sailboat was moored. But he didn't show up, although Lily waited half the night. She didn't blame him. They'd hardly said a word on the way home and when he pulled to the curb in front of Gram's rickety old house, Lily had practically jumped out of the taxi. She hadn't even bothered to say good-night.

The following morning Lily was wakened by Gram singing an African chant. Tossing aside the covers, Lily leaped from the bed and rushed into the kitchen.

Gram only sang in Swahili when things were looking up.

"Gram, what happened?" she asked excitedly, rubbing the sleep from her eyes. Two steps into the large central kitchen and Lily discovered Gram clothed in full African dress. Yard upon yard of bold chartreuse printed fabric was draped around her waist with deep folds falling halfway to the floor. The shirt was made of matching material and hung from her shoulders, falling in large bell sleeves. Wisps of bright-red hair escaped the turban that was wrapped around her head. Ten thin gold bracelets dangled like charms from each wrist.

"Gram." Lily stopped cold, not knowing what to think.

The older woman made a dignified bow and hugged Lily fiercely. *"Nzuri sana,"* she greeted her, ceremoniously kissing her granddaughter on the cheek.

Lily was too bemused to react. *"Nzuri sana,"* she returned, slowly sinking into a kitchen chair. Her grandmother might behave a bit oddly on occasion, but nothing like this.

Continuing to chant in low tones, Gram turned and pulled a hundred-dollar bill from the folds of her outfit and waved it under Lily's nose.

"Gram, where did you get that?" All kinds of anxious thoughts were going through her mind. Maybe Gram was so worried over their finances that she'd done something illegal.

Hips swaying, Gram crossed the room and chuckled. The unmusical sound echoed against the walls. "Bingo," she cried, and removed four more hundred-dollar bills.

"You won at bingo!" Lily cried, jumping up from the chair and dancing around the room. Their arms circled each other's waists and they skipped around the kitchen like schoolgirls until Lily was breathless and dizzy.

"You buy yourself something special," Gram insisted when they'd settled down. "Something alluring so those rich men at the Wheaton won't be able to take their eyes off you."

Lily did her utmost to comply. She left the house and spent the rest of the morning shopping. Half the day was gone by the time she'd located the perfect outfit. It was a silky black dress with a fitted bodice that dipped provocatively in the front, granting a glimpse of cleavage and hinting at the fullness of her breasts. Studying herself in the mirror, Lily turned sideways, one hand on her hips, and rested her chin on her shoulder as she pouted her lips. It was perfect. After paying for the dress, Lily hurried home. She rushed up to her bedroom and donned her new purchase, eying her reflection in the mirror. Jake would tell her if the dress had the desired effect. Besides, she owed him an apology.

His boat was in the slip at the marina when she arrived at the marina a short time later. Lily had never visited him without an invitation and felt uneasy about doing so now.

"Jake," she called from the dock. "Are you there?" The boards rolled slightly under her heels and Lily had to brace herself. "Jake," she repeated louder, hugging the full-length coat close to her.

"Coming." His tone sounded irritated and he was frowning as he stuck his head out from below deck. He stopped when he saw it was Lily and smoothed a hand through his thick hair. "Hi." Slowly he came topside. "What are you doing here? And why in heaven's name are you wearing that ridiculous coat?"

Lily glanced down over the long wool garment that had once belonged to Gram and felt all the more silly. "Gram won five hundred dollars at bingo last night. I bought a new dress and want your opinion on it. Can I come aboard?"

"Sure." Jake didn't sound nearly as eager as she'd hoped he would.

She lifted the gray wool coat from her shoulders and let it slip down her arms. "What do you think?" she asked. "Be honest, now."

One glance at Lily in that beautiful dress, and Jake could barely take his eyes off her. She looked sensational— a knockout.

"I...I didn't know if you'd want to see me," she continued.

"Why wouldn't I?" His answer was guarded, his words quiet. Still he couldn't take his eyes from her.

"I feel terrible about yesterday."

"It's no problem." He reached out his hand in silent invitation for her to join him and Lily deftly crossed the rough wooden dock to his polished deck.

"Gram insisted I buy something new. How do you like it?"

"I like it fine," he murmured, doing his best to avoid eye contact. "You look great, actually." That had to be the understatement of the century.

"Do you honestly think so?" she asked excitedly.

Jake smiled. "You look really nice."

"That's sweet," she said softly. "Thank you."

"Think nothing of it." With a sweep of his arm, he invited her below. "Do you want a cup of coffee?"

"Sure." She paused to remove her shoes and handed them to Jake. "Would you put these someplace where I won't forget them?"

"No problem." He went down before her and waited at the base of the steps in case she needed help. One bare foot appeared on the top rung of the ladder and the side split in the skirt revealed the ivory skin of her thigh as the next foot descended. Jake felt his heart constrict. He sighed with relief as she reached the bottom rung and turned around to face him, eyes sparkling. "I'll get you a cup," he announced, disliking the close confines of his cabin for the first time. Lily seemed to fill up every inch of available space, looming over him with that alluring scent of hers.

"How's the writing going?"

"Good." It wasn't. Actually he'd faced writer's block all day, and determined that it was Lily's fault. He didn't like what was happening between them and yet seemed powerless to stop it.

"Heard any more from Rex?"

"No." Lily slid into the tight booth that served as a seat around the kitchen table. "I won't see him again," she told him. "I promised you I wouldn't."

"Someone else will come along." And soon, he hoped. The quicker Lily found herself a sugar daddy, the better it would be for him.

"I know." She smiled up at him briefly as he set the mug on the table.

He didn't join her, fearing that if he slid into the seat beside her, they might accidentally brush against one another. And touching Lily while she looked so tempting in that dress shook Jake. It would be the attic all over again and he knew he wouldn't be able to stop himself. As it was now, he could barely tear his eyes from her. She lifted her mug and blew against the edge before taking a sip. Her dewy lips drew his gaze like a magnet. Jake turned around and added some sugar to his coffee.

"I didn't know you used sugar."

"I don't," he said, turning back to her.

"You just dumped three tablespoons into your cup." She sounded as perplexed as he felt.

Jake lifted one shoulder in a half-hearted shrug. "It must be something in the air."

"Must be," Lily agreed, not knowing what he was talking about. She dropped her gaze to the dark, steaming liquid. "I've been thinking that I need lessons on how to flirt."

Jake nearly choked on his coffee and did an admirable job of containing himself. Lily was so unconsciously alluring, that he couldn't believe that any man could ignore her.

"Will you teach me, Jake?" There wasn't anyone she trusted more. Jake had been all over the world and done everything she hadn't. Lily didn't think there was a thing he didn't know. With

that, he did choke on a mouthful of coffee. "Me?"

"Yes, you."

"Lily, come on. I don't know anything
about feminine stuff like that."

"Sure you do," she contradicted,
warming to her subject. "Every time
I bat my eyelashes at a man, I'm convinced he thinks I've got a nerve dis-
ease."

"Ask Gram."

"I can't do that." She waved her hand
dismissively. "Just tell me what Elaine
did that made you go all weak inside."

" I don't remember."

"Something like this?" She dropped
her eyes and parted her lips, giving him
her most sultry look.

Jake experienced a tenderness unlike
anything he'd ever known. He couldn't
teach her to flirt. She was a natural.
"Yeah," he murmured at last.

Discouraged, Lily straightened. Elaine

had known exactly what to do to make a man notice her. For months, Jake had been so crazy over the other woman that he'd hardly ever come by for a visit. It had shocked Lily when they'd split. Maybe Jake wasn't the best person to teach her what she needed to know. But she knew he wasn't immune to a woman's wiles. The problem was he thought of her as a sister. She could probably turn up on his dock naked and he'd barely notice.

"Forget it," she mumbled. "I'll ask Gram."

Three

Jake paced the small confines of his galley like a man trapped in an obligatory telephone conversation. He had to do something, and fast. Roughly he combed his fingers through his hair and caught his breath. Lily was beginning to look good to him. Real good. And that was trouble with a capital *T.* Either he found himself a woman, and quick, or…or he'd take it upon himself to find Lily a wealthy man. Both appeared formidable tasks.

If he involved himself in another relationship, it would surely end in disaster. No woman would be satisfied with his carefree lifestyle. Every woman he'd known, with the exception of Lily, had taken it upon herself to try to "save" him. The problem was, Jake didn't want to be redeemed by a woman's ambitions.

But locating a rich man for Lily wouldn't be easy either. It wasn't as if he traveled in elite circles. He had a few contacts—buddies from school—but he didn't know anyone who perfectly fit the wealthy profile Lily was after.

The only potential option was Rick, his friend from college days. From everything Jake had heard, Rick had done well for himself and was living in San Francisco. It wouldn't hurt to look him up and see if he was still single. Jake didn't like the idea, but it couldn't be helped.

Humming softly, Lily smiled at the doorman at the Wheaton and sauntered into the posh hotel as if she owned it. She was practicing for the time when she could enter a public place and cause faces to turn and whispers to fill the air. Lily felt good. The meeting with Jake hadn't turned out to be the confrontation she'd expected. Jake had every reason to be angry with her, and wasn't. If anything he'd behaved a bit weirdly. He'd seemed to go out of his way to be distant. When she was on one side of the boat, he'd stand on the other. He'd avoided eye contact as though he were guilty of something. The large bouquet of red roses on the piano was a nice surprise. A small white envelope propped against the ivory keys caused her eyes to widen, and her heart to do a tiny flip-flop. Lily knew without looking that Rex had sent the flowers. Her hands trembled noticeably as she removed the card and read the bold handwriting:

Sorry you couldn't make it, little filly. I'll see you next month on the 25th at nine.

Lily swallowed a nervous lump that clogged her throat. Next month or next year; it wouldn't make any difference. She'd given Jake her word and she wouldn't go back on it no matter how tempting. And tempting it was. Rex was interested. He must be, to send her the flowers and ask her out again.

With a heavy heart, Lily pulled out the piano bench and sat, her hands poised over the pearly keys before starting in on the same old songs.

As usual, Jake was waiting for her at the end of her shift. His gaze focused on the roses and narrowed fractionally.

"Daddy Warbucks?"

"Yeah." Lily didn't know why she felt so guilty, but she did. This was the first time in her life that anyone had sent her roses and she wasn't about to leave them at the Wheaton. "He's gone."

Jake felt a surge of relief wash over him. He wished that he felt differently about that Texan. It would have been the end of his troubles. Lily could have her rich man and he could go about his life without complications.

"He left a note with the roses, asking me out next month. Apparently he'll be back in town then."

"Are you going?"

The muscles at the side of her mouth ached as Lily compressed her lips into a tight line. "No."

"Good."

Maybe it was good for Jake, but Lily was miserable.

"Will I see you later?" she asked when he dropped her off in front of Gram's house.

"I'll be by."

Even with all his hang-ups about personal freedom and restricting schedules, Lily knew that if Jake said he'd be someplace, he'd be there eventually. Purposely waiting up for him, she sat watching the late-late show dressed in a worn terry-cloth housecoat that was tightly cinched at the waist. In an effort to stay awake, she sipped Marmite, a yeast extract, which had been stirred into hot water. Years ago while traveling in New Zealand, Gram had had her first taste of the thick, chocolate-like substance and she had grown to love it. She received the product on a regular basis from family friends now and spread it lightly over her morning toast. Lily preferred the dark extract diluted.

The movie was an old Gary Cooper one that had been filmed in the late nineteen fifties. Soon Lily was immersed in the characters and the plot and loudly blew her nose to hold back tears at a tender scene. A light knock against the front door announced Jake's arrival. She opened the door, waved him inside and sniffled as he took the seat opposite her.

Jake eyed her curiously. "You sick?"

Lily sucked in a wobbly breath and pointed to the television screen with her index finger. "No…Gary Cooper's going to be killed in a couple of minutes and I hate to see him die."

Jake scooted forward in the thickly cushioned chair and linked his hands. "I talked to an old friend today."

Lily's eyes didn't leave the black-and-white picture tube. "That's nice."

"Rick's a downtown attorney and has made quite a name for himself in the past few years."

Lily didn't know why Jake found it so important to tell her about his friend in the middle of the best scene of the movie.

Jake hated it when Lily ignored him. He couldn't imagine how she could be so engrossed in a film that made her weep like a two-year-old. "Lily," he demanded, "would you listen to me?"

"In a minute," she sobbed, wrapping a handkerchief around her nose and blowing. Tears streamed down her cheeks and she wiped them aside with the back of her hand.

Knowing that there wasn't anything he could do but wait, Jake settled back in the upholstered chair that had once belonged to a Zulu king and impatiently crossed his arms over his chest. He had terrific news to share—and she found it more important to cry over Gary Cooper than to listen to him. Ten minutes later, Lily grabbed the remote and turned off the TV. "That's a great movie."

"You cried through the whole thing," Jake admonished.

"I always cry during a Gary Cooper movie," she shot back. "You should know that by now."

Rather than argue, Jake resumed his earlier position and leaned forward in the chair toward her. "As I was saying…"

"Do you want a cup of Marmite?" Remembering her manners, Lily felt guilty about being such a poor hostess. Gram had taught her better than this.

"What I want," Jake said with forced patience, "is for you to sit down and listen to me."

Meekly lowering herself to the sofa, Lily politely folded her hands in her lap and looked at Jake expectantly. "I'm ready."

"It's about time," he muttered.

"Well. I'm waiting." Sometimes it took Jake hours to get to the point. Not that he did a lot of talking. He'd say a few words here and there and she was expected to get the gist. The problem was, Lily rarely did and he'd end up staring at her as if her head were full of holes.

"I saw Rick—my lawyer friend—this afternoon."

"The one from school?"

"Right. Anyway, Rick has become a regular socialite in the past few years and he's invited me to a cocktail party he's having Saturday night."

Lily blinked twice. She wouldn't have thought Jake would be so enthusiastic about a bunch of people standing around holding drinks and exchanging polite inanities. "That's interesting." She tried to hide a yawn and didn't succeed. Belatedly she cupped her mouth and expelled a long whiney breath.

Jake's face fell into an impatient frown. He didn't usually look that way until he was five minutes into his monologue.

"I thought you'd be thrilled," he murmured. It hadn't been easy to reach out to Rick—Mr. Success—and strike up a conversation after so many years.

"To be perfectly honest, I wouldn't have believed you'd enjoy a cocktail party."

"I won't. I'm doing it for you."

"For me?"

"There are bound to be a lot of rich men there, Lily. Undoubtedly some of them will be single and on the lookout for an attractive woman."

"What do you plan to do? Hand them my name and phone number?" she asked.

"You're going with me," he barked.

"Well, for heaven's sake, why didn't you say so?"

"Anyone with half a brain would have figured that out. You should know that I wouldn't be willing do something like this without an ulterior reason."

They stood facing each other, not more than two feet apart. The air between them was so heavy that Lily expected to see arcs of electricity spark and flash. Jake's breathing was oddly raspy. But then hers wasn't any better. They shouldn't be arguing—they were friends. Neither of them moved. Lily couldn't stop looking at him. They were so close that she could see every line in his face, every groove, every pore. Even the hairs of his brows seemed overwhelmingly interesting. Her gaze located a faint scar on his jawline that she'd never noticed before and she wondered if this was a souvenir from Iraq. He'd told her little of his experiences there.

His eyes were greener tonight than she'd remembered. Green as jade, dark as night, alive and glittering with an emotion Lily couldn't read. His mouth was relaxed and slightly parted as if beckoning her, telling her that she must make the first move. Surely she'd misinterpreted him. Jake wouldn't want to kiss her. They were friends—nothing more. What had happened in the attic had been a moment out of time and place. Still not believing what she saw, Lily raised her gaze to his and their eyes met and clashed. Jake did want to kiss her. And even more astonishing was that she wanted it, too. "Lily." He breathed heavily and turned away from her, stalking to the opposite side of the room. "I think I will have something to drink after all."

"Marmite?"

"Sure—anything."

Lily was grateful that she had something to occupy her hands and her mind. Jake didn't follow her into the kitchen, and she needed to have time to compose her thoughts. Good grief, what was happening to them? After all these months there wasn't any logical explanation why they should suddenly be physically attracted to each other. Something must be in the air—but spring was nine months away. A laugh hovered on her lips as she pictured tiny neon lights that flashed on and off across her forehead, telling Jake: *Kiss Lily.* But Lily knew it wasn't right. Jake was wonderful, but he wasn't the man for her. Thank heaven he'd had enough sense to turn away when he did.

Lily carried a steaming cup into the living room and carefully handed it to him. She wasn't so much afraid of being burned by the near-boiling water as she was fearful of her reaction if she touched him.

"I want you to attend that party with me." Jake picked up the conversation easily, pretending nothing had happened. Even though it was obvious they'd been a hair's breadth from hungrily falling into each other's arms.

"Saturday?" Her mind filled with niggling thoughts. She was scheduled to work, but she would be free at nine; she could wear her new dress. No, that was a bit too daring for a first meeting.

"Do you or don't you want to go?" Jake still hadn't taken a sip of his Marmite.

"Sure. I'll be happy to attend. Thanks for thinking of me." That sounded so stilted, Lily instantly wanted to grab back the words and tell him how pleased she was that he'd thought of her and was willing to help her out.

"I'll see you Saturday, then."

"Saturday," she echoed, and watched as Jake set aside his untouched drink and walked out of the house.

Lily didn't see Jake for two days. That wasn't as unusual as it was unsettling. It was almost as if they were afraid to see each other again.

During that time, Lily thought about

Jake. She didn't know what was happening, but it had to stop. Jake was the antithesis of everything she wanted in a man. He had no real ambitions and was perfectly content to live out his days aboard his sailboat, doing nothing more than write short stories that didn't pay. Usually he received three free copies of the publication in compensation for his hundred hours of sweat and toil. Sometimes Lily wondered why Jake wrote when each word seemed so painful for him. Jake was a paradoxical sort of person. He hid behind his computer screen and revealed his soul in heart-wrenching stories no one would ever read.

While Jake was perfectly content with his life, Lily desperately wanted to improve hers. She longed to explore the world, to travel overseas and dine in the shadow of the Eiffel Tower. She yearned to see China and lazily soak up the sun on a South Pacific island. And she didn't want to ever agonize over a price tag again. Bargain basements and second-hand stores would be forever behind her. But most of all, Lily never wanted to hear "Moon River" again.

On Saturday evening Lily dressed carefully. Her dark curls were swirled high on her head and held in place with combs her father had brought her from India when she was twelve. He'd died shortly afterward and Lily had treasured this last gift, wearing them only on the most special occasions. At the end of her shift, with the thirty-ninth rendition of "Moon River" ringing in her ears, Lily stepped out of the hotel, expecting Jake to meet her. She didn't see him, and for half a second, panic filled her.

"Lily," Jake said, stepping forward.

Lily blinked and placed her hand over

her heart at the sight of the tall, handsome man who stood directly in front of her. She squinted, sure she was seeing things. "Jake, is that you?"

"Who else were you expecting? Prince Charming?"

"You're wearing a suit!" A gray one that could have been lifted directly from the pages of *Gentlemen's Quarterly*, Lily realized in bemusement. The simple, understated color was perfect for Jake, emphasizing his broad shoulders and muscular build. "You look…wonderful!"

Jake ran his finger along the inside of his collar as if he needed the extra room to breathe properly. "I don't feel that way."

"But why?" She'd never seen Jake in anything dressier than slacks and a fisherman's bulky-knit sweater.

" I don't know. But knowing Rick, this

party is bound to be an elaborate affair and it's best to dress the part."

Lily could hardly take her eyes from him. He looked dashing. Her gaze dropped to her own much-worn dress. "Am I overdressed? Underdressed? I don't want to give the wrong impression." Her insecurities dulled the deep brilliance of her eyes.

Jake glanced at her and shrugged. "You look all right."

All right? She'd spent half the day getting ready, fussing over each minute detail. "I hope you know you're about as charming as the underside of a toad."

"Hey, if you want romance, try Hugh Jackman. I ain't your man."

"You're telling me!" she huffed.

"Are we going to this thing or not?" He held the taxi's passenger door open for her, but didn't wait until she was inside before walking around the front of the car.

The first ten minutes of the ride down Golden Gate Avenue past the Civic Center was spent in silence.

Lily felt obligated to ease the tension. Both were on edge. "I didn't know you owned a suit."

Jake's response was little short of a grunt. The expensive suit had been Elaine's idea. She was the one who'd insisted he needed some decent clothes. She had dragged him around town to several exclusive men's stores and fussed over him like a drone over a queen bee. He'd detested every second of it, but he'd been so crazy about her that he'd stood there like a stooge and done exactly as she dictated. His weak-mindedness shocked him now. In thinking over his short but fiery relationship with Elaine, Jake was dismayed by some of the things he'd allowed her to do to him. The last party he'd attended had been with Elaine. He'd sat back and listened as she introduced him to her phony friends, telling them that Jake owned his own company and lived on a yacht. To hear her tell it, Jake was a business tycoon. In reality, he owned one taxicab that he drove himself, and his "yacht" was a ten-year-old, twenty-seven-foot, single-mast, fore- and aft-rigged sailboat that most of Elaine's colleagues could have bought with their pocket change.

"Are you going to sit there and sulk all night?" Lily questioned, growing impatient.

"Men never sulk," Jake declared, feeling smug just as Rick's house came into view. Jake parked several yards away in the closest available space. His five-year-old Chevy looked incongruous on the same street with all the fancy foreign cars, so he patted his steering wheel affectionately as if to assure his taxi that it was as good as the rest of them.

Rick's house was an ostentatious colonial-style, with thick white pillars and a well-lit front entrance. Jake swallowed nervously. Old Rick had done well for himself, even better than Jake had assumed.

"It's lovely," Lily murmured, and sighed with humble appreciation. This was exactly the kind of home she longed to own someday—one with crystal chandeliers, Persian carpets and gold fixtures.

"Lovely if you like that sort of thing," Jake grumbled under his breath.

Lily liked it just fine. "Oh, but I do. Thank you, Jake."

The genuine emotion in her voice was a surprise and he tore his gaze away from the house long enough to glance her way.

"I should have been more appreciative. I'd never thought I'd be able to attend something as wonderful as this. Oh, Jake, just think of all the wealthy men who'll be here."

"I'm thinking," he mumbled, pleased for the first time that he'd accepted Rick's invitation.

If Lily was impressed with the outside of the house, she was doubly so with the interior. She resisted the urge to run her hand over the polished mahogany woodwork and refused to marvel at the decor for too long. A maid perfunctorily accepted their coats at the front door and directed them toward a central room where drinks were being served.

"Jake, old buddy."

Lily felt Jake stiffen, but was proud of the way he disguised his uneasiness and shook hands with the short man with a receding hairline. Lily could easily picture the man as a successful attorney. She could see him pacing in front of the jury box and glancing acrimoniously toward the defendant.

"Rick," Jake said with a rare smile. "It's good to see you. Thanks for the invitation."

"Any time." Although he spoke to Jake, Rick's gaze rested on Lily. "Jake, introduce me to this sweet cream puff."

"Rick, Lily. Lily, Rick."

"I'm most pleased to make your acquaintance," Lily murmured demurely. "Jake has told me so much about you."

Briefly, Rick's enthralled gaze left Lily to glance at Jake. "Where did you find this jewel?"

Lily's gaze pleaded with Jake to not tell Rick the real story of Gram confronting the Wheaton manager in full witch doctor's costume, outraged over Lily's starting wages. "We met at the Wheaton," Jake explained and Lily reached for his hand, squeezing it as a means of thanking him.

"Are you visiting our fair city?" Rick directed the question to her.

"No, I play the piano there."

"A musician!" Rick exclaimed. "I imagine you're a woman of many talents."

Jake didn't know what Rick was implying, but he didn't like the sound of it. He bunched up his fist until he realized that Lily's fingers were linked with his and he forced his hand to relax.

"Only a few talents, I fear," Lily answered with such self-possession that Jake wanted to kiss her. "But enough to impress my friends."

"Then I'd consider it an honor to be your friend."

Lily batted her lashes. "Perhaps."

From the way Rick's eyes widened, Jake knew that Lily had impressed his old friend. A surge of pride filled Jake and he struggled not to put his arm around Lily's shoulders.

Rick reached out to take Lily's hand. "Do you mind if I steal your girl away for a few minutes?"

Jake did mind, but this was exactly why he'd brought Lily to the party. She would make more contacts here than she would during a year of playing piano at the Wheaton. "Feel free," he murmured, lifting a glass of champagne from the tray of the passing server. He didn't watch as Lily and Rick crossed the room, Lily's arm tucked securely in the crook of Rick's elbow.

The bubbling liquid in the narrow crystal glass seemed to be laughing at him and, almost angrily, Jake set it aside.

He hated champagne and always had. He much preferred a hearty burgundy with some soul to it. He found an obscure corner and sat down, giving anyone who approached him a look that would discourage even the most outgoing party guest. He could hear Lily's laugh drift from another section of the house and was pleased she was enjoying herself. At least one of them was having a decent time.

Another waiter came past and Jake ordered Ouzo, a Greek drink. Gram had given him his first taste of the anise-flavored liqueur she drank regularly. Lily claimed it had made her teeth go soft, and to be honest, the licorice-tasting alcohol had curled a few of Jake's chest hairs. But he was in the mood for it tonight—something potent to remind himself that he was doing the noble thing. Now he knew how Joan of Arc must have felt as she was tied to the stake and the torches were aimed at the dry straw. No, he was being melodramatic again. What did it matter? He'd known all along that he was going to lose *his* Lily. But Lily wasn't his; had never been his. He drank down the liqueur with one swallow and felt it sear a path to his stomach. Lily was his good friend. He'd do anything for her and Gram—well, almost anything.

Jake asked for another Ouzo and drank it down with the same eagerness as the first. Another followed shortly after that. His eyes found a woman sitting on the sofa on the other side of the room, and she smiled. Hey, Jake mused, maybe this party wasn't such a loss after all. Maybe Lily wasn't the only one destined to have a good time.

He stood, surprised that a house as expensive as Rick's had a floor that swayed like a ship at sea. Suavely, he tucked one hand in his pants pocket and paused to smooth the hair along the side of his head. There wasn't any need to look like a slob.

Just when he was prepared to introduce himself to Goldilocks across the way, he heard the piano and stopped cold. "Moon River." Oh no. Rick had convinced Lily to entertain him. Jake knew how she felt about that song. Rick couldn't do that to Lily. Jake wouldn't let him. Rushing forward, he raised his hand and started to say something when the floor suddenly, unexpectedly, came rushing up to meet him.

Four

Holding a small bouquet of flowers, Lily traipsed through the hospital lobby to the open elevator, stepped inside and pushed the button for the appropriate floor. She'd worried about Jake all night. He'd looked so pale against the starched white hospital sheets. Pale and confused. Lily should never have left his side, but Rick had convinced her that there wasn't any more either of them could do. Jake had been given a shot and would soon be asleep. Nonetheless, Lily had lingered outside the hall until the shot took effect, then reluctantly left.

When the heavy metal doors of the elevator parted, Lily stepped out eagerly. She had so much to tell Jake. He'd been such a dear to have taken her to the party. Everything had turned out beautifully—except for his fall, of course. Lily had met several men, all of whom had an aura of wealth. She prided herself on her ability to recognize money when she saw it. Rick had insisted on buying her a new dress since the one she'd worn to the party had gotten stained. But Lily had adamantly refused. The dress wasn't ruined. Gram had used vinegar and a few other inventively chosen ingredients to remove Jake's blood.

Lily stepped past the nurse's station and headed down the wide hall to Jake's room. The faint smell of antiseptic caused her to wrinkle her nose. Jake would be glad to get out of there.

The door to his room was open and

Lily paused in the doorframe, looking at the nurse's aide who was stripping the bed of the sheets and blankets. Troubled, Lily's gaze slid to the number printed on the door for a second time to be sure she had the right room.

"Good morning," Lily murmured.

"Morning," the other woman answered flatly. "Is there something I can do for you?"

"Do you know where Jake Carson is?"

"Mr. Carson signed himself out early this morning."

Lily swallowed to relieve her voice of its shock and surprise. "Signed himself out? But why?"

"I believe Mr. Carson had several reasons, all of which were described in colorful detail."

"Oh, dear." Lily was shocked to realize she'd spoken out loud.

"I'm afraid so. He also insisted on

paying his own tab and wanted the bill brought to him immediately." Impatiently, the woman jerked the bottom sheet from the raised hospital bed. "I've seen a few stubborn men in my day, but that one takes the cake."

It didn't take much imagination for Lily to picture the scene. Jake could be a terror when he wanted to be, and from the frustrated look on the nurse's flushed face, Jake had outdone himself this time. Lily was all the more convinced that she shouldn't have left him. She shouldn't have listened to Rick. Next time, she'd follow her instincts.

"Did he say where he was going?" Lily pressed.

The woman hugged the sheet to her abdomen and slowly shook her head. "No, but I'm sure the staff could give you a few suggestions about where we'd like to see him."

"I am sorry." Lily felt obliged to apologize for Jake, although she was convinced he wouldn't appreciate it. "I'm sure he didn't mean…whatever it was he said."

"He meant it," the woman growled, placing the sheet with unnecessary force inside a laundry cart at her side.

"Well, thank you, anyway," Lily stammered. "And here…" She shoved the small bouquet of daisies into the woman's hands. "Please take these." With that, Lily turned and hurried from the room.

By the time she arrived back at Gram's, Lily was more worried than before. "Gram, Jake's left the hospital."

Gram stood at the ironing board, pressing dried flowers between sheets of waxed paper. "I know."

"You know!"

"Why yes. He called earlier."

"Where is he?" Lily demanded, the wobble in her voice betraying her concern. "He shouldn't be alone...not with a head injury."

"He sounded perfectly fine," Gram contradicted, moving from the iron to the stove where she stirred the contents of a large stockpot.

"Is he at the marina? I should probably go there, don't you think? Something could happen." Not waiting for a response, Lily made a sharp about-face and headed out of the kitchen. For a panicked second, she imagined a dizzy, disoriented Jake stumbling about the sailboat. He could slip and fall overboard and no one would know.

"It'd be a waste of time."

"A waste of time? Why?" Lily paused and turned around to face Gram, her thoughts scrambled.

Humming an old Beatles tune, Gram

continued stirring. "Jake's on his way over here."

"Now?"

"That's what he said."

"Why didn't you tell me that earlier?" Lily cried.

Gram turned away from the stove and studied Lily with narrowed, knowing eyes. "You seem worried, girl. Jake can take care of himself."

"I know…but he's lost a lot of blood. He had ten stitches and…"

"He's not going to appreciate it if you make a fuss over him."

Lily forced the tense muscles in her back and shoulders to relax. Gram was right. Jake would hate how concerned she was.

"What else did he say?" Trying to disguise how disquieting Lily found this entire matter, she pushed the kitchen chair under the table.

"Do you want some split-pea soup?" Gram asked as though she hadn't heard Lily's question.

"No, thanks." An involuntary grimace crossed her face. Gram loved split-pea soup, but Lily didn't know why she would be eating it in the middle of the morning.

A loud knock against the front door announced Jake's arrival. Lily battled the urge to run across the room to meet him.

Jake let himself inside. "Morning."

"Hello, Jake." Lily laced her fingers in front of her. "How are you feeling?"

"Great," he answered, breezing right past her and into the kitchen.

"Soup's ready," Lily heard her grandmother tell him.

"I appreciate it, Gram."

"When it comes to restoring a person's health, it's better than chicken noodle."

"Anything you cook is better than my futile attempts."

Shocked and a little hurt at Jake's abrupt greeting, Lily stood stiffly, half-way between the kitchen and the front door. Jake may have said only one word to her, but his eyes spoke volumes. Over the past year they'd often informed her of what he was thinking and feeling before he could say a word. They were a stormy shade of jade when he was angry, and that seemed to be happening on a regular basis lately. At other times they were a murky green, but that was generally when he was troubled about something. Then there were rare times when they sparked with what seemed a thousand tiny lights. They'd glittered like that when he'd first seen her in the dress she'd bought with Gram's bingo winnings and again later, when they'd met before Rick's party. But then they'd quickly changed to that murky shade of green. Lily didn't know what to make of that. Jake had been so easy to read in the past, but either he was changing or she was losing her ability to understand the one man she thought she knew so well.

"How are you feeling?" Lily asked for the second time, coming into the kitchen.

Jake pulled out a chair at the table, and sat drinking Gram's soup from a ceramic mug.

"Fine," he answered curtly.

"You look better." Some color had returned to his face. Yet he remained so pale that the tiny creases around his eyes were more noticeable than ever.

Gram joined Jake at the table, pouring two additional servings of soup.

"Here." She gave one to Lily who wrinkled her nose at it.

"No thanks, I prefer chicken noodle."

Jake's snort was almost imperceptible. "I'll be ready in a minute here," he added.

Lily glanced at Gram, who appeared oblivious to the comment. "Ready for what?" Lily inquired.

"Shopping."

"You're going shopping?" Good grief, he'd just been released from the hospital. "Whatever for?" If he needed anything, she'd be happy to make the trip for him.

"We're going out."

"Us?"

Jake caught Gram's eye. "You didn't tell her?"

"I didn't get a chance."

"Tell me!" Lily demanded, not liking the way Jake was ignoring her.

"Jake's taking you out to buy you a new dress," Gram informed her.

"The dress is fine," Lily protested loudly. "Didn't you tell him that?"

"I did," Gram huffed. "But he insists."

Jake's gaze bounced from Gram to Lily and back again. "Did you tell Lily that it won't do any good to argue with me on this one? I saw what I did to her dress. I'm buying her another one and that's all there is to it."

Lily sank into the chair across from Jake and boldly met his gaze. "In case you hadn't noticed, I'm standing right here. There's no need to ask Gram to tell me anything when you and I are separated by less than two feet." The words came out sharp and argumentative despite her effort to sound casual.

"If you insist." Gram chuckled. "You two remind me of Paddy and me."

Paddy was Lily's grandfather. He'd died several years before Lily was born, but the tales Gram told about him were very telling of the deep love and commitment her grandparents had shared. Lily hoped to find the same deep and lasting love with her own husband.

"You ready?" Jake asked, standing.

Lily looked at Gram for support, then back to Jake. "I hate to have you spend money on me. It isn't necessary."

"Would you like it better if Rick bought you a dress? Is that it?"

"Of course not." She hardly knew Rick and didn't want him buying her clothes.

"Then let's get this over and done with." He was halfway across the living room before Lily moved.

"Gram, what's wrong with Jake? He's not himself."

Gram shook her pin-curled head and laughed. "I can't say I rightly know, but I have my suspicions."

With Jake marching ahead, Lily had little choice but to follow him. He was sitting in the driver's seat of his taxi and glaring impatiently toward Lily as she came down the front steps.

"How'd you get your cab back?" she asked, opening the car door. They'd left it parked in front of Rick's house and Lily had wondered if Jake wanted her and Gram to pick it up for him. That was one of the things she'd planned to ask him that morning at the hospital.

"I have my ways," he grumbled, checking the side-view mirror before pulling onto the street. A heavy pause followed. "Did you have a good time last night?"

The question repeated in Lily's mind. Had she? Yes and no. The evening had been one she'd dreamed about for years. She'd met several interesting men who might be worth her time. Rick had been a gentleman, kind and considerate and genuinely concerned when Jake had fallen. He'd taken charge immediately and knew exactly what to do. Lily had been surprised at her own response to Jake's injury. She'd fallen to pieces, and Rick had been there to lend his support.

"Hello? Earth to Lily," Jake said. "Did you or did you not have a good time?"

"The evening was grand. Thank you, Jake, for inviting me."

"Did you meet someone?" Anticipating her answer, his grip tightened around the steering wheel. He wanted Lily to assure him that she had found the rich man of her dreams. But in the same breath, he wanted her to tell him she'd found no one.

"Not really."

"What about Rick?"

"He was very nice."

The corner of Jake's mouth curved up sarcastically. Her word choice was comforting. "Anyone else?"

"Not really. A couple of others said they planned to visit the Wheaton to hear me play, but I don't think they'll show."

"Who?" Jake demanded.

Lily lifted one shoulder in a delicate

shrug, surprised that Jake would sound angry when meeting eligible wealthy men was the reason he'd taken her to the party. "I don't remember their names."

"If they do come, I want to know about it so I can have them checked out." He was eager to know for other reasons as well—ones that weren't clearly defined in his mind. He wanted Lily married and happy and he wished to heaven that he could forget the taste of her. Every time he looked at her, he had trouble not kissing her again. He'd received a head injury, Jake told himself. One that was apparently affecting his reasoning ability. He shouldn't be thinking of Lily in that way. His only option was to set her up with Rick or one of the others—and quickly.

"Jake," Lily said softly.

"Yes?" He swallowed hard.

"Why are you insisting on buying me a dress?"

"What's the matter? Do you think Rick could afford a better one?"

"Oh, Jake, of course not."

From the soft catch in her voice, Jake knew he'd hurt her to even imply such a thing. "It's a matter of pride," he explained. "You told me Rick wanted to replace the one I ruined. My blood stained it, so I should be the one to buy you another dress."

"But Gram got the stain out."

"It doesn't matter."

"But…"

"I'm buying you the dress. Understand?"

She didn't answer.

"Understand?" he repeated forcefully.

"Repeaters is off Thirty-second."

"What?"

"The secondhand store where I usually

buy my dresses." It took all of her will-power to give in to his pride. Jake had always been so reasonable, but his harsh tone told Lily she'd best concede grace-fully. Either Jake would go with her or he'd buy something for her on his own.

"I'm not getting you anything second-hand."

"All right," she agreed reluctantly. "Either Sears or Penney's is fine."

"We're going to Neiman-Marcus."

"Neiman-Marcus, Jake!" Lily's jaw fell open. Jake couldn't afford to shop there.

The announcement was as much of a shock to Jake as it was to Lily. He'd driven toward downtown, thinking they'd figure out where to shop once he'd found parking. But now that he'd spoken the words, he wouldn't back down. If he was going to buy Lily a dress, it would be one she'd remember all her life.

"I saw a dress I liked on display in Penney's." Her hands felt clammy just at the thought of spending all Jake's money on some silly dress. He worked too hard and saved so little.

"And I saw one at Neiman-Marcus," Jake countered. "You're always talking about how you want to shop there someday. I'm giving you the chance."

A hundred arguments crossed her mind as they parked and Jake escorted her through the elite department store.

"Jake," Lily pleaded.

"And nothing on sale." Jake paused in front of a mannequin. "Nice," he said to no one in particular.

"It should be," Lily informed him stiffly, reading the price tag. "This little piece of chiffon is fifteen hundred dollars."

It demanded all of his discipline for Jake to bite his tongue. Fifteen hundred dollars for a dress? He had no idea. He hesitated a second longer. "So?"

"Jake, honestly, fifteen hundred dollars would wipe you out." Lily was growing more uneasy by the minute. This whole idea was ridiculous. Pride or not, Jake had no business buying her clothes. Not here.

"May I help you?" An attentive salesclerk approached them.

"Yes," Jake insisted.

"No," Lily countered.

"Perhaps if I came back in a few minutes." The salesclerk took a step in retreat.

"My friend here would like to try on this dress," Jake said, lifting the hem of the pricey dress on the mannequin.

"Jake," Lily hissed under her breath.

"And a few more just like this," Jake continued.

The clerk gave a polite nod. "If you'll come this way."

Jake's hand on the small of Lily's back urged her forward.

"Do you have any color in mind?"

"Midnight blue, red, and maybe something white." The choices came off the top of his head. Once, a long time back, it had occurred to him that with Lily's dark hair she'd look like an angel in white.

"I have just the thing." The clerk motioned toward the dressing rooms on the other side of the spacious floor.

Like a small duckling marching after its mother, Lily walked behind the salesclerk through rows and rows of expensive dresses.

Sitting in a deep, cushioned chair outside the dressing room, Jake leaned against the padded back and crossed his legs, playing the part of a generous benefactor. This was just the type of thing Rick would relish. Jake had recognized the look in Rick's eyes the minute he laid eyes on Lily. He'd wanted her. Jake knew the feeling. He'd wanted Elaine from the first minute he'd seen her; had lusted after her and been so thoroughly infatuated with her that he couldn't think straight. But Lily was different. She wasn't Elaine—knowledgeable in the ways of the world and practiced in controlling men. No, Lily was an innocent.

Changing positions, Jake uncrossed his legs and folded his arms over his chest. He didn't know what could be taking so long—or how he was going to pay for whichever dress Lily chose. But it would be worth it to salvage his pride.

"Jake," Lily whispered, coming out of the dressing room. She wore a deep-blue dress with a scalloped collar and short sleeves. "How do you like it?"

Jake watched her walk self-consciously in front of him. It was a dress, nothing special. "What do you think?" he asked.

"The saleslady called it Spun Sapphires."

"It has a name?"

"Yes." She inserted her hand inside the thin belt. "It's a little big around the waist."

"Then try on another."

Relieved, Lily returned to the dressing room. The dress was nice, but she hated the thought of Jake spending nine hundred dollars on it. As tactfully as possible, she asked the clerk to bring dresses that were in a lower price range. Eager to please, the woman returned with a variety in the colors Jake had requested. A white crepe frock with feminine tucks and simulated pearl embellishments caught her eye.

Jake felt a little too conspicuous as he sat and waited. Since Iraq he liked to think of himself as an island, an entity unto himself. His life was comfortable. He needed no one. There were no ties to the mainland, no bridges, no sandbars. Nothing. Elaine had been the first to tug him closer to the shore. And now Lily... Just when he wanted to cast thoughts of her from his mind, he glanced up to discover her standing in front of him. She was breathtakingly beautiful in a simple, white dress. He felt the air constrict in his lungs. Without realizing what he was doing, he slowly rose to his feet. Their eyes met for an instant before Lily turned away. Jake could hardly breathe, let alone speak. He'd never seen anyone more lovely.

"What's this one called?" He swallowed and held his breath, trying to slow his racing heart. The task was impossible. Lily was a vision; she was everything that Jake had ever wanted in a woman. His fingers ached with the need to trace her cheekbones and touch the fullness of her lips.

"It's called Angel's Breath," she said.

"We'll take it," Jake informed the salesclerk, without glancing her way. Tearing his eyes away from Lily was unthinkable. He wanted to hold the memory of her in his mind and carry it with him for the remainder of his days.

"But you don't even know how much it is," Lily objected.

"The price doesn't matter." Her nose was perfect, Jake decided, with a soft sprinkling of freckles across the narrow bridge. He adored every single one.

Jake paid the salesclerk while Lily changed back into her clothes. The woman smiled warmly at him as he signed the credit card receipt for three hundred and sixty-five dollars. On Lily it would have been a bargain at twice the price.

"That dress is gorgeous on your wife," the salesclerk told him with a sincerity Jake couldn't doubt. It wasn't until they were at the car that Jake realized he hadn't corrected her. Not only was she not his wife, but he was doing everything he could to marry her off to a wealthy man so she could have everything she desired. When the time came, he'd let her go without regret. When the time came...but not today.

"Thank you, Jake," Lily told him once they were outside the store.

He looked down at her, captivated by the warmth of her smile. "Any time." He reached for her hand, linking their fingers. "Are you hungry?"

"Starved. But it's my turn to treat you. What would you like?"

"Food."

"That's what I love most about you," Lily teased. "You're so articulate." The word *love* echoed in the corners of her mind, sending a shaft of sensation racing through her to land in the pit of her stomach. They took the cable car down to Fisherman's Wharf and stood in line with hordes of tourists. Lily's favorite part of San Francisco was the waterfront. The air smelled of saltwater and deep-fried fish. The breeze off the bay was cool and refreshing. They ate their lunch on the sandy beach behind the Maritime Museum. Lily took off her sandals and stepped to the water's edge, teasing the tide and then retreating to Jake's side when the chilly water touched her toes. For his part, Jake leaned back against the sand and closed his eyes. Lily's musical laugh lulled him into a light slumber. He was content with his world, content to have Lily nearby. He thought about the characters in the short story he'd recently submitted to the *New Yorker*. Lily had claimed it was his best story yet and had encouraged him to dream big. Personally, Jake thought it was a waste of time but to appease her, he'd sent it to the prestigious publisher.

"Jake?"

"Hmm?"

Lily sat at his side, drawing up her legs so that her arms crossed her knees. "It's almost four."

"Already?" He sat up. The day had slipped past too quickly.

"You're not working tonight, are you?"

Lily hesitated. "No." Jake knew her schedule as well as she did.

"Good." He settled back on the sand, folding his arms behind his head. "I'm too relaxed to move."

"Me too," Lily said with a sigh and

joined him, lying back in the sand. They were in such close proximity and Jake squeezed his eyes shut at the surge of emotion that burned through him at the merest brush of her leg against his. Slow, silent seconds ticked past, but Lily didn't move and Jake hadn't the will. The summer air felt heavy with unspoken thoughts and labored heartbeats. It demanded everything within Jake not to reach for Lily's hand. He felt so close to her. His heart groaned. Lily wasn't Lily to him anymore, but a beautiful, enticing woman. "Jake?"

He rolled his head to the side and their eyes met,. Her warm breath tickled his face. "Yes?"

"I've enjoyed today."

"Me, too."

"Can we do it again?"

Jake turned his head and stared into the clear blue sky. For a long minute he didn't say anything. He couldn't do this again and remain sane; having Lily this close and not touching her was the purest form of torture. But he could never be the man she wanted. "I don't know." He would be doing them both a favor if he got out of her life and moved further down the coast. That was the nice thing about owning a sailboat and driving a taxi; he didn't have a string of responsibilities tying him down.

"You're right," Lily concurred. "It's probably not a good idea."

"Why?" Something perverse within him insisted that he ask.

"Well…" Lily hedged. "Just because."

"Right," he agreed. "Just because." Standing up, Jake wiped the granules of sand from his clothes. "I think I should take you home."

"You probably should." But Lily's tone lacked enthusiasm. The day had been charmed, a gift she had never expected to receive. "Gram will wonder about us."

"We might cool her wrath if we bring a peace offering," Jake suggested.

"What do you have in mind?"

"Chinese food."

"But, Jake…"

"Gram loves it."

"I know, but—"

"No buts."

They took the cable car back to where Jake had parked his taxi. Lily tried to talk to him twice on the way through Chinatown. Jake knew his way around, popping in and out of shops, greeting friends and exchanging pleasantries along the way, and all the while ignoring Lily.

"I didn't know you spoke Chinese," Lily commented, hurrying after him.

"Only a little." He didn't mention that half of everything he'd said had been an explanation about Lily.

"Not from what I heard."

"I'm a man of many talents," he joked,

loading her arms with the brown paper sacks that contained their meal.

Again on the way home, Lily tried to talk to Jake, but he sang at the top of his lungs, infecting her with his good mood. Soon Lily's sweet voice joined his. At a stoplight, their smiling eyes met briefly and the song died on his lips. Without thinking, Jake leaned over and touched his lips to hers. His hand brushed the hair from her temple and lingered in the thick dark strands.

A blaring horn behind him rudely alerted Jake of the fact that the light had changed. Forcing himself to sing again, Jake stepped on the accelerator and sped ahead.

Lily had a more difficult time recovering from the casual kiss. Had that really just happened? It somehow felt so right to have Jake claim her lips as if he'd been doing it for a lifetime. His light touch left her longing for more.

When Jake glanced at her curiously out of the corner of his eye, she forced her voice to join his, but it wasn't the same and both of them knew it.

Jake eased to a stop in front of the house. Gram was standing on the front porch, her hands riding her round hips as she paced the small area. "It's about time you got home, girl. Rick called. He's on his way over."

Five

The sensation of dread went all the way through Jake. He'd known from the minute they entered Chinatown that Lily had been trying to talk to him. But in his stupidity, Jake feared that she was going to mention things he didn't want to discuss—mainly that something rare and special was happening between them. Such talk was best delayed and, if possible, ignored entirely.

"Rick's coming?" he questioned, turning to Lily and trying to disguise the raging battle that was going on inside him. Rick was better for Lily than he'd ever be. Rick could give her the world. But Jake didn't like it. Not one bit. There was something very wrong about spending the day with Lily and then watching her march off with Rick that evening. His gut instinct told him Rick was wrong for Lily, but he couldn't say anything without making a fool of himself. He'd been doing enough of that lately as it was.

"I tried to tell you earlier," she mumbled, feeling guilty. "I...we...Rick and I, that is, we're going to dinner..."

"No problem," Jake said, feigning a shrug of indifference. "Gram and I will have a good time without you." He walked ahead of Lily and took the older woman by the hand. "I guess you're stuck with me tonight."

"I'd consider it a privilege," Gram said with a smile.

Jake responded with one of his own. He led the way into the house, carrying the sacks of spicy Chinese food to the kitchen. If Lily wore the white dress he bought her, he didn't know what he'd do. She couldn't. Not after all they'd shared that day. Deep down, Jake knew she wouldn't do that to him.

Lily walked to her room with all the enthusiasm of someone going to the dentist for a root canal. She felt terrible. Everything had been so perfect today with Jake. When they'd stopped at the red light and Jake had kissed her, Lily had died a little. The kiss had felt so right— as though they were meant to be together forever. Only they weren't.

Taking her new dress from its box, Lily hung it in her closet. She wouldn't wear it for anyone but Jake. It was the most beautiful article of clothing she'd ever owned and she'd treasure it for the rest of her life.

After checking the contents of her

meager closet, Lily chose a midi-length straight black skirt and matching top. She dressed hurriedly, then took a moment to freshen her makeup and run a brush through her tangled hair. She'd just finished when the doorbell chimed. A glance at her watch confirmed that he was right on time.

Gram was introducing herself to Rick when Lily appeared.

"Lily." Rick looked at her appreciatively and stepped toward her. Claiming both hands, he kissed her lightly on the cheek.

Lily had to resist wiping his touch from her face. She hadn't found it offensive, only wrong. It wasn't Jake who was kissing her and it felt unnatural. "Hello, Rick." Automatically, her gaze shifted to Jake, who had just emeged from the kitchen.

Rick's eyes followed hers. "Glad to hear you're okay after that fall, Carson."

"Yeah, thanks." Jake's reply was as abrupt as a shot.

"I'll be home early," Lily told Gram, hoping to avoid a confrontation between the two men.

Rick's hand curved around the back of Lily's neck. "But not too early."

At the front door, she turned to Jake. "Thank you for today."

He pretended not to hear her and strode back into the kitchen. He didn't like her going out with Rick, but he hadn't said a word.

"Jake doesn't mind you dating me, does he?" Rick asked when they reached his car. He drove a Mercedes convertible. Lily had often dreamed of riding in one with the top down and the wind whipping through her thick hair. Now that she was standing in front of one, she couldn't seem to muster the appropriate level of enthusiasm.

"No, he doesn't mind," she told Rick.

"I don't want to horn in on you two if you've got something going. But from what Jake said..."

"There's nothing between us," Lily said, fighting the heavy sadness that permeated her voice. "We're only friends." *And then some*, she added silently. But the *some* hadn't been defined.

"Did I tell you where we were going?" Rick asked next, politely opening the car door for her.

"No."

"The Canlis."

Her returning smile was weak. "Thanks. Sounds fantastic."

They arrived at the popular restaurant a half-hour later. From everything she'd read, Lily knew the Canlis was highly rated and extremely expensive. For the first time she'd have the opportunity to order almond-saffron soup. Funny, now that the time had arrived, she'd have given almost anything to sit at the kitchen table across from Gram and Jake and struggle with the chopsticks Jake insisted they use to eat pork-fried rice.

"You have heard much about this place?" Rick asked.

"Oh, yes. From what I understand, the food's wonderful."

"Only the best for you, Lily. Only the best."

Rick took Lily out for two evenings straight. On Sunday night, following their dinner at the Canlis, he took her to the Cliff House and ordered champagne at three hundred dollars a bottle. After years of scrimping by with Gram for the bare necessities, Lily discovered her sense of priorities was offended by seeing good money wasted on something as frivolous as overpriced champagne.

When she mentioned it to Gram later, her grandmother simply shook her head. "Did it taste better than the cheap stuff?"

"That's the problem," Lily admitted, and sighed dejectedly. "I don't know. I've had champagne that was plenty good at a fraction of the cost."

"Rick must want to impress you."

Lily's gaze fell to her lap. "I think he does." Rick wined and dined her and claimed he found her utterly refreshing. He called her his "sunbeam" and was kind and patient. Lily should have been in ecstasy to have someone like Rick interested in her. She liked him, enjoyed his company and looked forward to seeing him again; but something basic was missing in their relationship— something that Lily couldn't quite put her finger on.

On Monday evening Jake was waiting outside the Wheaton for her as usual. A warm smile lit up Lily's dark eyes as she spotted him from the lobby, standing outside his taxi.

"Hello, Jake," she said, walking toward him, her heart pounding.

"Lily." He uncrossed his long legs and slowly straightened. "How'd it go tonight?"

"Good." About as good as it ever goes, playing the same songs night after night.

"Meet any more rich Texans?" He forced the joke when the last thing he felt was cheerful.

"Not tonight."

"How did everything go with Rick?" Jake had thought of little else over the past two days. It felt good to be responsible for giving Lily what she wanted most. And wretched because it went against his instincts. But Rick was a decent sort. He'd be good to Lily.

"Rick's very nice."

"I knew you'd like him."

"I do." But not nearly as much as I like you, she added silently.

"Where'd he take you?"

"The Canlis."

"Rick always did have excellent taste." Most especially in women, Jake thought to himself. His friend wasn't going to let Lily slip away. She was a priceless gem, rare and exquisite, and it hadn't taken Rick long to covet her. Jake couldn't regret having introduced them; he'd planned it. But he hadn't expected that letting Lily go would be so difficult.

"How'd the writing go today?"

"Pretty good. I've got a story for you to read when you have the time." He reached inside the cab for a manila envelope and handed it to her.

Pleased, Lily hugged it to her breast. "Is there anything special you want me to look for?"

"The usual."

"Have you heard anything back on that one you sent to the *New Yorker*?"

Jake snickered and shook his head. "Lily, I only sent it there to please you. Trust me, the *New Yorker* isn't going to be interested in a story from me."

"Don't be such a defeatist. Who can say? That story was your best. I liked it."

The corner of his mouth edged up in a self-mocking grimace. "You like all my stories."

"You're good, Jake. I just wish..."

"What?" He opened the passenger side for her and walked around the front of the vehicle.

"I think you ought to think about novels," Lily told him, once he was seated beside her.

"Maybe someday," he grumbled.

The evening traffic was lighter than usual as Jake drove the normal route to Gram's in the Sunset district. They didn't talk much after Lily suggested Jake consider writing novels. Ideas buzzed through his mind. Maybe he ought to think about it. Almost always the characters in his stories were strong enough to carry a book-length story. Naturally it would call for more plot development, and that could be a problem, but one he could work at learning. To his surprise, he found the idea appealing.

Lily studied the man sitting on the seat beside her. His gaze was centered on the street, his dark-green eyes narrowed in concentration. Sensing Lily's gaze, Jake turned toward her.

"Are you coming in tonight?"

Mentally Jake weighed the pros and cons. He liked talking over his day with

Lily and Gram. They offered him an outlet to the everyday frustrations of life. Yet, coming around every night the way he used to could mean problems. The day they'd gone shopping proved that. But did he really need to worry with Gram around? "If you don't mind?"

Lily laughed, surprised that he'd even suggest such a thing. "Of course I don't mind. You're always welcome. You know that."

He smiled then until the emerald light sparkled in his eyes and Lily discovered she couldn't look away. "Yes, I suppose I do," he said finally.

By the time Jake returned it was after eleven. Lily sat in the living room with Gram. She'd read over Jake's short story and made several markings on the manuscript. Every time she read something of Jake's she was stirred by the powerful emotion in his stories. This one was particularly heart wrenching. The story involved a grumpy old man who lived alone. He had no women or children in his life, but he had a soft spot in his heart for animals. Late one night, the crotchety old man found a lost dog that had been frightened and had nearly drowned in a bad storm. He brought the dog, a miniature French poodle, into his home and fed it some leftovers. As he worked at drying off the dog, he complained gruffly that Miss Fifi, as he'd named her, deserved to be left out in the storm. The little dog ignored the surly voice and looked up at him adoringly with dark eyes. She was so grateful to have been rescued that she followed the old man around the house. Soon she was sleeping on the end of his bed and working her way into his crusty heart. People who saw the man with the fancy poodle were amused by the sight of them.

The old man felt torn. Miss Fifi was a damn nuisance and he definitely didn't like drawing attention to himself. Yet every day, he grew more attached to the dog. At the end of the story he found her a good home and, without a second thought, went about his life as before.

Lily was sitting on the sofa with her feet tucked up under her when Jake knocked once before letting himself inside.

His gaze fell to the manila envelope. "Did you read it?"

"Yes."

Gram was swaying in her rocker, watching the news. She acknowledged Jake and returned her attention to the television set.

"Well?" He shouldn't have let her read it. Lily was frowning. The story wasn't one of his best. He should have ditched it. He sat on the end of the coffee table and leaned forward, resting his elbows on his knees.

"You're getting better and better," she hedged. "The best thing about your writing, Jake, is that you're a natural storyteller."

"But?" He could tell she was leading up to something unpleasant by the way her eyes avoided his. "But...the ending's wrong."

"What do you mean?"

"The little dog loved that lonely old man."

"He wasn't lonely."

"But he was!" Lily protested. "That's the reason the old man came to love the dog so much. He longed for companionship."

"You're thinking like a woman again. The old man liked his life. He was content. He didn't need anyone or anything."

"But he loved that fancy dog."

"And people laughed at him." His gaze centered on her breasts and he cursed himself for being so weak.

"Why should he care what people think? He didn't like them anyway. You've set him up to be so antisocial. The only friend he's got is that dog."

Smiling sadly, Jake shook his head. "That crusty old man knows that dog isn't right for him. He's doing the only thing he can by giving her to someone who will appreciate and love her."

"*He* appreciates and loves her," Lily countered hotly.

"But he isn't right for her. He loves her, but he knows he has to let her go. You missed the point of the story."

"I didn't miss it," Lily told him shortly. "It's right here, hitting me between the eyes. That old man, who you want the reader to see as strong and fiercely proud, is actually shallow and foolish."

"Shallow and foolish?" Jake spat the words back at her. "He's noble and unselfish." It astonished him that Lily, who was generally so intuitive, could be so off base in her assessment.

"Let's agree to disagree," he proposed.

"It won't sell, Jake."

"So? I've got tons of stories that'll never see a printed page."

"But this one could, if you'd change the plot around."

"I'm not changing a thing."

"That's your choice." She folded her arms over her chest and stared past him to the picture on the wall. Any other time Jake would have taken her feedback to heart. Usually he appreciated her insight and made the changes she suggested, but she was wrong about this one.

"Yes, it is my choice," he said through gritted teeth.

A heavy silence settled over them.

"Would you like a glass of Marmite?" Lily asked five minutes later, seeking some way to smooth matters over. She was uncomfortable when things weren't right between her and Jake.

"Sure." Jake followed her into the kitchen. "You disappoint me, Lily."

"I do?" She hesitated before returning the teakettle to the stove. "How?"

"With the story. You're thinking like a woman and forgetting that this is a man's story."

"Women buy the majority of magazines."

"Maybe."

"Maybe nothing—that's a fact. And what's so wrong with thinking like a woman? In case you hadn't noticed, I *am* one."

Oh, he'd noticed all right. Every time she moved in that T-shirt she was wearing, he noticed. From the instant he'd walked in the door, her breasts had enthralled him, pressed against the thin material of her shirt, round and full. Stalking to the other side of the room, Jake swallowed tightly and forced his gaze in the opposite direction.

"The fact is," Lily continued, "I don't much like the hero in your story."

"I thought we were through discussing the story."

"You were the one who brought it up."

"My mistake." Jake ground his teeth in an effort to hold her eye and not allow his gaze to drop.

"What are you two shouting about?" Gram asked, joining them.

"Jake's story."

"Nothing," Jake countered, and at her fiery gaze, he added, "I thought we agreed not to discuss it."

"Fine." Lily's arms hugged her waist.

"You two sound like snapping turtles."

"We aren't going to argue anymore, Gram," Lily promised.

"The way you two have been carrying on lately, one would think you were married. Me and Paddy sounded just like the two of you. We'd fight, but then we'd make up, too. Those were the best times," she chuckled. "Oh, yes, making up was the best part."

"We aren't fighting," Lily insisted.

"And there isn't a snowball's chance in hell that we'd ever marry," Jake barked angrily.

Involuntarily, Lily winced. She was surprised by how much his words hurt her. "You aren't exactly my idea of good husband material, either."

"Of course I'm not," Jake growled. "You're like every other woman—you want someone who can run a four-minute mile after a fast buck."

"And what's wrong with that? A girl

can dream, can't she? At least I'm honest about it." Lily battled to hold on to her temper, pausing to take several deep breaths. "Maybe it would be best if I didn't read your stories anymore, Jake."

"You're right about that," he declared, marching into the living room. He jerked the manila envelope off the coffee table with such force he nearly knocked the table over. "Damn right," he said again on his way out the front door.

The screen door slammed and Lily cringed, closing her eyes.

"More and more, the two of you sound like Paddy and me," Gram announced a second time.

Lily's answering smile was nearly nonexistent. She and Jake weren't anything like Gram and Paddy. Her grandparents shared a mutual trust and a love so true that it had spanned even death.

Unshed tears brightened Lily's eyes as

she turned off the lights one by one and went to bed.

The next evening Jake wasn't outside the Wheaton when Lily was finished for the night. Standing in the lobby she looked out at the long circular driveway and she'd hoped they would have a chance to talk. But Jake was angry, probably angrier than he'd ever been with her. Lily couldn't stand it. Their friendship was too important to let something as petty as a short story stand between them.

Feeling dejected, Lily secured her purse strap over her shoulder and walked into the cool evening air. She was at the end of the long driveway when she recognized Jake's cab barreling down the street. He eased to a stop along the curb beside her.

Her heart leaped at the sight of him. Jake leaned across the front seat and opened the door. "Are you talking to me?"

"Of course."

"Climb in and I'll give you a ride home."

Lily didn't hesitate. "Jake…"

"No, let me go first. I apologize. You were right about the story. I don't know what was wrong with me."

"No," she said in a hurried breath. "I was the one who was wrong. I've felt wretched all day. We shouldn't fight."

"No, we shouldn't." He grinned at her then—that crooked, sexy grin of his that melted her insides—and reached for her hand. "Let's put it behind us," Jake suggested.

Lily smiled and felt the tension of the last twenty hours drain from her. "What did you do with the story?"

"I trashed it."

"But Jake, it was a good story. With a few changes, I know it would sell."

"Maybe. But I wasn't willing to

change the ending. The best place for it was the recycling bin."

"I wish you hadn't."

"Friends?" he questioned.

"Friends." Jake may have given up on the story, but they'd learned something about each other in the process. Their friendship was important. Whatever else happened, they couldn't discard what they shared.

Her regret over the discarded story persisted as Jake drove her home, but she bid him goodnight and raced up the walk toward the house.

"Rick called," Gram told Lily when she walked in the front door.

"Okay." Lily stood at the window, watching Jake drive away. "Jake and I are friends again."

"Were you enemies before?"

"No, but we had a fight and now that's over."

"And you fretted about it most of the day."

"I was worried," Lily corrected, releasing the drape so that it fell against the window. "I don't like there to be tension between Jake and me."

"I know what you mean. I felt the same way when Paddy and I fought."

Lily remained at the window long after Jake had driven out of sight. Rick was waiting for her to phone back and Gram was walking around comparing Lily and Jake to her and Paddy. They weren't anything alike. Jake and Lily were friends…and then some, her mind echoed…and then some.

"Gram, how do I look?" Lily had swirled her hair high atop her head and put on a striking red dress.

"As pretty as a picture," Gram confirmed without looking up from the crossword puzzle she was working on.

"Gram, you didn't even look."

"But you're always pretty. You don't need me to tell you that." She yawned loudly, covering her red lips with a veined hand. "You seeing Rick or Jake tonight?"

"Rick." She hoped the lack of enthusiasm wasn't evident in her voice.

"You don't sound pleased about it."

It did show. "We're going to the opera."

"You'll love that."

Rick had managed to obtain tickets to Mozart's *Così Fan Tutte*, which was being performed by the Metropolitan Opera Company from New York. From what little Lily knew, the performance had been sold out for months. She didn't know how Rick had managed it. He'd mentioned it once in passing, much to her delight, and the next thing she knew, he had tickets.

"It's something I've always wanted to do," Lily agreed. She was fascinated by the costumes and extravagance. Rick would be the type of husband who'd take pleasure in taking his wife out and buying her huge diamonds and an expensive wardrobe. Lily forced a smile. Those things had been important to her for so long, she hated the thought of doing without them. But Rick deserved someone who would love him for who he is and not what he could provide.

The sound of footsteps pounding up the cement walkway snapped Lily out of her daydream.

"Lily!" Jake burst in the front door and grabbed her by the waist. His handsome face was flushed and his emerald eyes sparked with excitement.

"I just heard back from the *New Yorker*. They want my story!"

"Oh, Jake!" She threw her arms around his neck and gleefully tossed back her head, squealing with delight.

Jake lifted her from the carpet and whirled her around until they were both dizzy.

"Plus they're actually paying me," he added. He set her back on the carpet but kept his arms around her. Nor did her hands leave his shoulders as she smiled up at him, her eyes filled with warmth and happiness.

"I knew it would sell," she told him. "I knew it."

Jake felt he had to either let go of Lily or pull her to him and kiss her senseless. Reluctantly, he chose the former and turned to Gram who was sitting in her old rocker, swaying.

"Nzuri sana," Gram cried, resorting

to the happy Swahili word to express her congratulations.

Jake bent down and kissed the older woman soundly on the cheek. "We're celebrating. All three of us. A night on the town, dinner, dancing. No more beer and television for us."

Lily's heart sank all the way to her knees. "When?"

"Right now." Jake paused, seeming to notice her dress for the first time, and sobered. "You're going somewhere." There was no question in his voice. He knew. The joy bubbling inside him quickly went flat.

"To the opera with..."

"...Rick," he finished for her. He rammed both hands into his pants pockets and gestured outwardly with his elbows. "Listen, that's not a problem. We'll do it another time."

"I don't want to do it another time."

"It works out this way sometimes,"

Jake announced. "Don't worry about it." He headed out the door.

"Gram?" Lily turned frustrated, unhappy eyes to her grandmother and cried. "What should I do?"

"That's up to you, girl," Gram answered obliquely.

"Jake—" Lily rushed out the door after Jake. "Wait up." The screen slammed and Lily hurried down the stairs of the porch.

Jake paused in front of his cab, keys in hand. "What?"

"Don't go," she pleaded.

"From the look of you, Rick will be here any minute."

"Yes, but I want to go with you."

"For as long as I've known you, you've talked of wanting to attend an opera. You're going. We'll celebrate another time."

"But I want to be with you."

"No."

Lily battled with herself. She couldn't wait. Jake deserved this celebration. This sale was a victory, a triumph. Ever so briefly, Jake had held her with an exhilaration that would fade in time. She wanted to be with him tonight more than anything—more than seeing an opera or sharing almond-saffron soup with Rick.

"Please, please come back in three hours," she pleaded, holding his hand. "I'll be waiting for you." Because she couldn't stop herself, Lily stood on her tiptoes and planted a warm, heartfelt kiss on the side of his mouth.

Six

"Are you sure you're going to be all right?" Rick asked with such tender concern Lily thought she might cry.

In response, she pressed her palms against her stomach and leaned her head against the headrest in the luxury car. "I'm sure it's nothing serious."

"I should have known you weren't feeling well." Rick's gentle voice was tinged with self-derisive anger. "You haven't been yourself all evening."

Because Lily had felt guilty all evening!

"You've been so quiet."

It wasn't like her to deceive anyone!

"I only wish you'd said something earlier."

She couldn't. When she had asked Rick to take her home because she wasn't well, Lily had felt as if there were a neon light identifying her as a scheming liar flashing across her forehead.

When Rick parked the Mercedes in front of Gram's, Lily automatically looked around for Jake's cab. She saw no sign of it and didn't know whether to be grateful or concerned.

Rick climbed out of the car and crossed over to her side, opening her door. He gave her his hand and studied her with worried eyes. "You're so pale. Are you sure you don't want me to stay with you?"

"No," she cried quickly, perhaps too quickly. "But thank you, Rick, for being so good to me." Her lashes fluttered against her cheek as she dismally cast her gaze to the sidewalk.

"I hope to be good to you for a very long time," Rick announced softly, slipping an arm around her waist and guiding her toward the house. "I never imagined I'd find someone like you, Lily."

The stomach ailment Lily had invented became increasingly more real. Her insides knotted. They paused on the porch and Rick tucked a finger under her chin, raising her eyes to his. Ever so gently, he brushed his mouth over her cheek. "Can I see you next week?"

Lily would have agreed to anything if it would help lessen her intense feeling of guilt. "If you'd like."

"Oh, I'd like, my sunbeam, I'd like it very much." With that he tenderly lifted the hair from her forehead and kissed her again.

Lily had the physical response of a rag doll. She didn't lift her hands to his shoulders or encourage him, but Rick didn't appear to care or notice.

"I'll call you in the morning," he promised. Within a minute, he was gone.

Like a soldier returning to camp after a long day in the field, Lily marched into the house. Gram was asleep and snoring in her rocking chair. The crossword puzzle had slipped unnoticed to the floor. Gently, Lily shook her grandmother.

"Come on, Gram, let me help you into bed."

Gram jerked awake with a start. "Oh, it's you."

"Who were you expecting?"

"Jake. You did say he was coming back, didn't you?"

"Yes…but he isn't here."

"He will be," Gram stated confidently, sitting upright. She rubbed a hand over her eyes and looked around her as though half expecting Jake to be there without either of them noticing. "Trust me, girl, he'll be here."

Lily wasn't as certain. He hadn't actually agreed to come back, but he hadn't told her he wouldn't either. Lily had been the one to convince Jake to submit it to the *New Yorker*. They should be celebrating together.

Lily changed out of her evening gown and into the white dress that Jake had bought her. A night as significant as this one demanded a dress that was just as special.

Pausing at her bedroom window, Lily parted the drapes and stared into the starlit sky. The street was empty and her heart throbbed with anticipation. If Jake didn't come, she didn't know what she'd do. Perhaps go to his boat. Tonight he wouldn't escape her.

A half-hour later, Lily sat in the still living room, staring silently at the elephant tusks that adorned the wall. The moving shadows cast by the trees outside, dancing in the moonlight, seemed to taunt her for being so foolish.

Gram's last words before heading to bed were that Jake would come. The sound of Jake's cab registered in her mind and she bolted to her feet, sucked in a calming breath and rushed to the door. He was really there. She was standing on the porch by the time he'd parked. He didn't look eager to see her and stopped the instant he realized she was wearing the dress. When he started toward her again, he trod heavily—like someone being led to a labor camp.

"Gram said you'd come." She rubbed her hands together to dispel her nervous energy.

Jake spread his fingers wide in a gesture that told her he hadn't wanted to return. But something stronger than his will had led him back to her.

"What did you tell Rick?" Jake stood on the sidewalk as if he wasn't quite sure he wanted inside.

"That I wasn't feeling well."

"And he bought that?"

"By the time we left the opera, it was true."

"And how are you feeling now?"

"Terrible." She hung her head so that her hair fell forward.

"I shouldn't be here."

Why did Lily have to look so beautiful standing there in the moonlight? She was miserable and confused and it took everything in him not to reach for her and haul her into his arms and comfort her. Rick had probably wanted to do that. Involuntarily, Jake's fist clenched. The thought of Rick holding Lily produced such a rage within him that he felt like smashing his hand through a wall. "I'm glad you came back," Lily said softly.

Her intense gaze commanded his attention, and Jake knew he could refuse her nothing.

"I'm glad I did too," he admitted with reluctance, walking toward her.

"It's a little late for going out to eat. I thought…that is, if you don't mind…that we could order a pizza."

"With anchovies?"

Her eyes lit up with a smile. "Only on your half."

"Agreed." He took the stairs two at a time and paused at the darkened living room. "Where's Gram?"

"She fell asleep. I'll wake her."

"No." A hand on Lily's forearm stopped her. No, tonight was for them. "Let her rest."

"All right."

She smiled at him and Jake felt his stomach twist. If he had any sense left, he'd get out of there right away. But the ability to reason had left him the first time he'd kissed Lily that night in the attic. From that minute on he'd behaved like a fool. He'd like to blame Lily for what he was feeling, but he couldn't. With her, everything had been of his own making.

"I brought some wine." Actually he'd left it in the front seat of the cab. He hadn't been sure he'd be staying. "I'll be right back."

Lily had the wineglasses out by the time he returned. She turned to him when he walked into the kitchen and Jake found he couldn't look away from her no matter how hard he tried. "Do you want a corkscrew?"

Lily's words shook him from his trance. "Yeah, sure." He paused to clear his throat. "You look nice in that dress." That had to be the understatement of the year. She was the personification of the very name of the gown: Angel's Breath—so soft and delicate. It was the purest form of torture to be near her and not touch her.

Lily handed him the corkscrew and while he fiddled to open the wine bottle, she casually browsed a pizza flyer she grabbed from the side of the fridge. "Should we pick the pizza up ourselves or have it delivered?"

"That's up to you."

"Have it delivered." Lily didn't want to go out again or do anything that would disrupt the evening. "What toppings do you want?"

"Anchovies, pepperoni, olives, green pepper—" he paused "—and sausage. What about you?"

"Cheese," she told him, and laughed

at the doubtful look on his face. "I'm just teasing. I'll have the same except for those disgusting little fish."

The cork came out of the wine bottle with a popping sound and Jake filled both glasses. "Here."

Lily accepted the wine and took a small sip. It was excellent. "This is good."

"I wanted something special."

She touched the edge of her wineglass to his. "To Jake: a master of words, a skilled storyteller, a man of obvious talent and virtue."

"And to Lily, who lent me her support."

"Moral and immoral," she added with a small laugh.

"Mostly moral."

Together they tasted the wine and then moved into the living room to sit on the zebra skin beside the wide ottoman. Lily had a fleeting thought to suggest they light a fire in the fireplace, but the evening was warm. "Thank you, Lily, for all your encouragement."

"Thank you, Jake, for being such a talented storyteller."

"To friendship." His eyes didn't leave hers.

"To friendship," she repeated in a hushed whisper.

They each drank their first glass and Jake replenished their supply.

"Jake."

"Hmm?"

"What really happened between you and Elaine?"

The question was so unexpected that his mouth parted, searching for words. "What do you want to know for?"

She lifted one shoulder and lowered her gaze to the red liquid. "You were so close to her."

"Yeah. So?"

"And then everything blew up."

"She wanted me to be something I couldn't."

"But that's part of what's great about you, Jake. You're so versatile. You can do anything."

"But only if I want to." Jake had no qualms about his talents. He'd tried enough things in life to know what Lily said was true. He wasn't being egotistical in admitting as much, only honest.

With a lazy finger, Lily drew imaginary circles over the top of her wineglass. "Were you lovers?"

"What?" Jake sat up so quickly that the wine nearly sloshed over the sides of his glass. "What kind of question is that?"

"I just want to know." Morbid curiosity had driven her to ask.

"That's none of your business." He

downed the remainder of his glass in one giant swallow. "Do you mind if we don't talk about Elaine?"

"All right." Already Lily regretted having brought up the other woman. It was a sore subject. But Lily couldn't regret that Jake had broken things off with Elaine. She wasn't nearly good enough for him.

"What about you and Rick?"

She straightened. "What about us?"

"Has he kissed you?"

Lily clamped her upper teeth over her bottom lip and hunched her shoulders. "Sort of."

"How does a man 'sort of' kiss you?"

Lily rose to her knees, planted her hands on his shoulders and slanted her mouth over Jake's. "Like this," she whispered, gently grazing his mouth with hers. Their mouths barely touched in a soft caress.

Jake nearly choked on his own breath as a shaft of desire shot through him. He broke contact and leaned back, lowering his gaze. Lily was achingly close; she smelled like summer and sunshine and everything good. He had to look away, fearing he'd feel compelled to toss aside the wineglass and pull her into his arms. "Yes, well, I see what you mean."

"You knew Rick was married before, didn't you?"

"I seem to remember something about that."

"He's been divorced less than a year."

"What happened?" Jake didn't care two cents about the breakup of Rick's marriage, but he needed the distraction. Anything to take his mind off how badly he wanted Lily. "I'm not exactly sure, but apparently she left him for another man."

"That must've hurt." The remark was

inane, but every second was torture having Lily so close.

"He's insecure and lonely."

"So are a lot of people."

Lily rotated the stem of the wineglass between her thumb and fingers. "I know."

"You like Rick, don't you?" Jake pressed. His gut feeling that Rick wasn't right for Lily persisted, but he wouldn't say anything. Not after what happened with that oil-rich Texan. Jake was beginning to doubt that anyone would ever be good enough for Lily.

"He's a nice man."

"Rich."

Softly, Lily cleared her throat. "Yes, he seems to be."

"That's what you wanted."

Lately, Lily wasn't so sure. She set the wineglass aside, got up, and moved to the window to stare into the night. The city lights obliterated the brilliance of the stars, but Lily was only pretending to look into the sky.

Jake joined her, coming to stand behind her. He raised his hands to cup the gentle curve of her shoulders and rested his cheek against the side of her head. "It's a beautiful night, isn't it?" He shouldn't be touching her like this, even in the most innocent way. Her nearness was a stimulant he didn't need. She smelled much too good for his sanity. Rick could give her all the things he'd never be able to afford. A knot of misery tightened in his chest.

"Yes, it's lovely," she mumbled. Without meaning to, she leaned back against Jake. He accepted her weight and slid his hands down the length of her arms. Desperately he wanted to hold her—to touch her without giving in to the temptation to kiss her. Lily was meant to be cherished and treasured, and he couldn't do her justice. Lily didn't move, barely breathed. The light touch of Jake's hands stirred her blood. She yearned to turn and have his arms surround her. The taste of his mouth lingered on hers unbearably.Without thinking, Jake turned his face into her hair and breathed in the fragrance of her shampoo. He lowered his face and nuzzled her ear. Lily tilted her head, luxuriating in the warm sensation that flooded through her.

"Lily," Jake breathed desperately. "I shouldn't be holding you like this."

"I like it."

"I do too. Too much."

"But I want you to hold me."

"Lily, please."

"Don't hold me then," she murmured. "Let me hold you." Without warning, she turned and slipped her arms around his waist and pressed her ear against his heart.

"Lily."

"It feels good in your arms," she purred, tightening her grip so that he couldn't break the contact. "How can it be wrong when it feels this good?"

"I don't know. Oh, Lily…" He whispered her name as he lowered his head, searching out her mouth. He touched his lips against hers, savoring her. She tasted like melting sugar, unbearably sweet and highly addictive.

Restlessly she moved against him, caught up in the moment as her passion for him took over.

"Lily," he pleaded against her mouth. "Hold still. We shouldn't let things get out of hand."

"I can't help it." She combed her fingers through his hair and looked up at him with wide, adoring eyes. "This feels so right."

"Lily…"

"Shh," she whispered and planted her mouth over his. She wound her arms around his neck and caressed his mouth with hers. "Your kiss is irresistible."

"So is yours." He paused to study the desire in her eyes. They were playing a dangerous game, which they both stood to lose. Yet he was unable to resist and he lowered his mouth to capture hers again.

Lily moaned softly, her lips moving against his. A low groan slipped from Jake's throat and he forced deeper contact, gripping the sides of her face and fusing their mouths together.

He came away from her weak, his resolve diminishing by the second. He hugged her hard, struggling deep within himself to find the willpower to release her. With a superhuman effort, he broke contact, stepping back and holding her at arm's length. "The wine went to our heads."

Her small smile contradicted his words. "We didn't have that much."

"Obviously more than we should have."

"I like what you do to me."

"Well, I don't like it," he hissed. "Tonight was a fluke and best forgotten."

"I'm not going to forget it."

"Well, I am. This isn't going to happen again. Do you understand? It's not right."

"But Jake…"

"I'm leaving. Right now,. If you have half the intelligence I credit you with, you'll forget this ever happened." He dropped his arms, and rubbed a hand over his face. "Goodnight, Lily."

She could hardly see him. Salty tears clouded her vision. "Goodnight, Jake." He was gone before she could utter another word.

"Morning." Gram greeted Lily cheerfully the following day. "I see Jake came. I told you he would."

Lily pulled out a kitchen chair and sat. After a restless, unhappy night she wasn't feeling very motivated.

"Yes, he was here."

"You coming down with a cold, girl? Your eyes are all red like you were awake half the night."

Lily blinked and offered her grandmother a feeble smile. "I think I might be."

Gram pushed a handful of vitamins and herbal supplements in Lily's direction. "You better start taking these."

"All right."

Gram gave her an odd look as Lily downed each capsule without argument. "I see you two celebrated with some wine."

Her explanation was mumbled. "Jake brought it."

"Where'd he take you for dinner?"

They had never gotten around to ordering the pizza. "We...we just had the wine."

"Ah," Gram muttered knowingly. "So you sat around and talked."

Lily pulled out the chair and stood in front of the old porcelain sink, her back to her grandmother. "Yes, we talked." Her fingers tightened around her mug. They'd talked, and a lot more. It was the "lot more" that would be difficult to explain.

"What did Jake have to say?"

"This and that." Nervously, Lily set the mug on the long counter. "I think I'll go get dressed."

"You do that," Gram said with a knowing chuckle. "Me and Paddy used to talk about 'this and that' ourselves. Some of our best conversations were spent discussing those very things."

On Monday evening Jake wasn't parked in his usual spot outside the

Wheaton when Lily finished her shift. She lingered around the lobby for an additional fifteen minutes, hoping he'd arrive and they'd have a chance to talk. He didn't. And he wasn't there the next evening, either. Lily didn't require a typed message to know that Jake was avoiding her. Maybe he felt they needed a break from each other to give ample thought to what had happened. But Lily would have felt better if Jake hadn't been playing a silly game of hide-and-seek with her.

Early Wednesday evening, Rick appeared in the lobby of the Wheaton and sat listening to Lily play. He clapped politely at the end of a series of numbers. No one applauded her playing; she was there for mood and atmosphere, not as entertainment.

When she had finished, Lily slid off the polished piano bench and Rick rose to join her.

"You're very gifted," he said, kissing her on the cheek.

"Thank you."

"Would you like a cocktail?"

Lily hesitated. She wanted to check if Jake was out front. If he was, Lily had everything she wanted to tell him worked out in her mind. She had no intention of mentioning what had happened over the wine. She'd decided that she'd play Jake's game and pretend the alcohol had dictated their uncharacteristic behavior. She planned to be witty and clever and show him that she hadn't been nearly as affected by his kiss as he seemed to believe. Playing this role was a matter of pride now. "Let me tell Jake first," Lily told Rick.

"Sure." A guiding hand at her elbow led her through the hotel and into the foyer. "Why do you need to talk to Jake?"

"He usually gives me a ride home."

"Every night?" Rick uttered a faint sound of disapproval. "I wasn't aware that you saw Jake that often."

"That's how we got to be such good friends." Lily stood between the two sets of thick glass doors, scanning the long circular driveway. Jake wasn't there. Her heart sank.

"Apparently he can't tonight."

"Apparently not."

"I'll take you home. For that matter, there isn't any reason why I can't see you home every night. I hate the thought of you having to rely on Jake's schedule for a ride home."

"I'm not relying on Jake's schedule. He's here when he can be, and not here when it's inconvenient or he's got a fare. The agreement works well for us both." Perhaps she did depend more on Jake than she should. But Jake would be as offended as she to have Rick suggest as much. "And as for you seeing me home every night, that's ridiculous."

"But I want to take care of you," Rick protested, his arm closing around her waist. "Let's go have that drink and we'll talk it over."

"There's nothing to discuss." Now Rick was irritating her. She didn't want to have a drink with him; she wanted to talk to Jake. Only Jake wasn't around and hadn't been for three days. Lily missed him. She hadn't realized how much she shared with Jake—nonsensical things about her day that only he would understand.

By Saturday afternoon, Lily was irritable and snapping at Gram. Rick had declared that he was coming to listen to her again and Jake continued to avoid her. Lily couldn't recall a time in all her years when she felt more frustrated.

"I haven't seen Jake around lately," Gram complained as Lily pulled weeds from the front flower beds. Alongside her, Gram groomed her African violets, smiling under a huge straw hat with a brightly colored bandanna wrapped around the brim.

"He's been busy." With unnecessary force, Lily jerked a weed free of the soft soil. "I haven't seen him for an entire week."

"Not since you two discussed 'this and that'?" Gram asked with a knowing glance.

"Nope." The cool earth felt good against Lily's hands. For once she didn't care if there was grit and grime under her manicured nails. Everything felt different after what has happened with Jake. "Gram, what would you say about me changing jobs?"

"Changing jobs? But I thought you

liked it at the Wheaton. Or is it Jake that's worrying you?"

"Jake hasn't got anything to do with it."

"This decision seems sudden."

"Forget it, then. I'll stay at the Wheaton and play 'Moon River' for the rest of my life. I don't care if I ever see Jake again." The minute the words escaped her lips, Lily realized what she'd said, and snapped her mouth closed.

"Seems to me that you're more worried about seeing Jake than you are about playing that song."

Lily kept her mouth shut. She had already said more than she'd intended.

"Why don't you just pay him a visit?" Gram asked, undaunted.

"Should I?" Lily's first inclination was to hurry to the marina, but she had her pride to consider. Already it had taken a beating, and Lily doubted it could go another round.

"I can't see what harm it'd do."

To Lily's burdened mind it could solve several problems. To hell with her pride! "Maybe I will drop by and see how he is. Perhaps he's been ill or something."

"He could even be waiting for you to come."

Lily sat back on her haunches and brushed a stray curl from her face. A thin layer of mud smeared her cheek. "All right, I'll do it."

By the time Lily had showered and changed clothes, she had grown nervous and fidgety. Maybe going to Jake's wasn't the best idea, but Lily couldn't stand the terrible silence any longer.

On her way to the marina, she made a stop to order the pizza they hadn't gotten around to eating that other night. Carrying the thin cardboard box in both hands,

Lily walked down the long, rolling dock to where his sailboat was moored.

"Jake!" Her voice trembled as she called out his name.

Below deck, Jake heard Lily calling for him and quickly closed the story he was writing on his laptop.

Seven

Jake's heart sped up at the sound of Lily's voice. He got up slowly, unsure of what he should do. He'd avoided her all week and with good cause. After what had happened at their "victory celebration," they needed to stay away from each other.

Besides, he reasoned, Lily didn't need him anymore; she had Rick. Jake had seen Rick's car at the Wheaton nearly every evening. He still couldn't reconcile himself to Lily's dating the guy. But he had no one else to blame. He'd introduced them. He couldn't protest at this point. He was snared in a trap of his own making. The best thing for him to do was make himself scarce.

"Jake, I know you're in there," Lily called again.

Jake's fist clenched at his side and an irritated noise slipped from deep inside his throat. If he didn't react it would be just like that stubborn woman to hop on board the *Lucky Lady* and search him out. Then he'd look like even more of a fool than he did already. Reluctantly, he climbed on deck.

"Hello, Jake," Lily began.

He tucked in his shirttails, giving the impression that he'd been preoccupied. "Lily."

"Did I catch you at a bad time? You weren't asleep, were you? Gram thought you might be sick."

His gaze just managed to avoid hers. "This is a bit of a bad moment. I'm busy."

"Oh." She dropped her gaze. "I brought a pizza. We…the other night we forgot about it."

"We didn't exactly forget it," he corrected her. "We just didn't get around to ordering it." His eyes delved into hers. Already it was happening. He couldn't help noticing how beautiful she was standing there with those huge brown eyes, looking betrayed and hurt.

"Anyway, I thought I could bring a pizza now."

Jake shifted his gaze to the flat box in her arms.

"But if you're busy, I'll understand." She didn't, not really. He must realize that coming here had cost her a lot of pride. The least he could do was make it easier on her.

Something in her voice reminded Jake that this wasn't any less difficult for Lily. It ws wrong of him to protect his ego at her expense. "It was thoughtful of you to come."

The tension eased from Lily's shoulders as Jake stretched out his hand to help her aboard. The boat rocked gently as she shifted her weight from the narrow dock to the *Lucky Lady*.

"There are anchovies on your half." She smiled up at him and Jake knew instantly that he was in trouble.

Lily drew in a long breath as though she didn't know what to say now that she was aboard the boat.

"It looks like rain, doesn't it?" she suggested, casting a discerning eye toward the thick gray clouds. "Maybe we should take this below."

Jake's chest tightened. Being alone with Lily was bad enough, but the thought of being next to her in the close confines of the cabin was almost more than he could bear.

"Jake?"

"Yeah, sure." He led the way and Lily handed the pizza down to him before expertly maneuvering the few steps that led below deck.

"Have you been working on another story?" Lily asked as she spied his laptop. Crumpled yellow sticky notes littered the tabletop and filled what limited space there was in the dining area. "It looks like you're having a few problems. Do you want to tell me your plot? That helps, sometimes."

Setting the pizza beside the tiny sink, Jake cleared away his mess. "No," he answered starkly.

Lily was taken aback by his answer. For a minute neither spoke.

"Why not?" Lily asked, trying to sound curious instead of hurt. Jake often talked out his plot ideas with her and listened to her reactions. Invariably, he argued his point and then, more often than not, accepted her suggestions.

"Every writer comes to the time when he has to break away…"

Lily sighed and shook her head regretfully. "Why are you so angry with me?"

"I'm not." The words came quickly.

"I thought we were friends, and all of a sudden you're treating me like I'm your worst enemy."

"I'm not mad."

"I haven't seen you in a week. Friends don't avoid each other like that'."

"I've been busy." Even to his own ears, the excuse sounded lame.

"Friends are honest with each other," Lily continued.

"I haven't lied."

"Friends tell each other what's on their minds."

"Nothing's bothering me. Why can't you accept that?"

Lily made a tsking noise that sounded remarkably like Gram when she was displeased about something.

"All right," Jake countered. "You want to talk about being friends? Fine. Then maybe you should think about what's been going on between us. You may be innocent, Lily Morrissey," Jake retorted, "but you're not naive enough to believe that friends kiss the way we do." Hoping to give the appearance of nonchalance, Jake leaned against the counter and crossed his arms. "I don't like what's happening."

"Nothing's happening," Lily said, struggling to keep her voice from rising. "We aren't any different than we were six months ago."

"Oh, I beg to differ!"

"All right, I concede that our relationship has gone to a deeper level, but we're still good friends. At least that's what I'd like to think."

Jake snorted. "We're in serious trouble."

"You're being overdramatic. I...I like kissing you. You make me feel warm and tingly inside. I just don't think that's wrong."

"Not wrong; bad."

"You're only saying that because you think kissing me will lead to something more."

Jake looked nonplussed. "And it doesn't?"

"Not if we don't want it to."

"Lily." Her name came out in a rush of breath as if he were reasoning with a young child. "Kissing is only the first step. The next thing you know, we'll be in bed together and wondering how we let things go so far."

"You seem to be equating a simple

friendly kiss with love and marriage. Good grief, Jake. We're friends and we just happen to like to kiss each other. It doesn't have to lead to anything."

"If we don't stop thinking like this, the next thing I know I'll be shopping for diapers."

Lily laughed. "Honestly, Jake, you make it sound far more dreadful than it is. Here, let me show you." She moved across the narrow confines of the cabin and placed her hands on his shoulders.

Jake stiffened and jerked away as if her touch burned him. "No."

"It's only a kiss, not a hand grenade."

"I don't think we should be kissing."

"But I want to prove something." Her voice was small and she couldn't keep the disappointment out of it. Before Jake had the opportunity to react, she moved her mouth against his in a soft caress.

Jake felt liquid fire seep through him.

"See?" Lily announced proudly. "And I'm not humming the 'Wedding March' or anything. From everything Gram's told me, there isn't the slightest possibility of my getting pregnant from a kiss."

The thoughts Jake was having didn't have anything to do with marriage and a family. His gaze fell past her to the small area where he slept. He thought about sleeping with Lily at his side and seeing her hair spread out on his pillow. The vision of her lying there without clothes and reaching her arms out to him nearly ate a hole right through him.

"Right," he grumbled.

"To further prove the point, I think we should do it again."

"I don't know." He closed his eyes, knowing that one pleading glance from Lily and he'd give her anything she wanted. He hated his lack of self-control. It had never been like this with other women. He had always been the one calling the shots. Jake opened his eyes to discover Lily standing so close that all he had to do was lean forward and their bodies would touch. He could feel the heat radiating from her. So little would be required of him to press his thigh to hers, to feel her breasts against his chest. His senses were suddenly awake to her every curve and it was slowly driving him insane.

Unable to keep his hands away, Jake tenderly cupped her cheek. Her thick lashes fluttered closed as she turned her face into his palm. Ever so gently, she kissed the inside of his hand. The inch or so between them was eliminated before another second could pass. They stood thigh to thigh, breasts to chest, and feasted on the feel of each other. With a reverence that shocked him, Jake lowered his head and claimed Lily's mouth.

Their lips met in the sweetest, most profound kiss Lily had ever experienced. Passion smoldered just beneath the surface, but this was a different kind of kiss—one that Lily didn't know how to define. Her hand crept up his chest and closed around the folds of his shirt collar as she clung to him.

When Jake lifted his mouth from hers, Lily smiled up at him and tears clouded her eyes. "That was beautiful," she whispered.

"You're beautiful." He tucked a strand of hair around her ear and traced her temple with his fingertips.

She had that dreamy look of a person in love.

Lightly, he kissed her again. "Lily, believe me when I tell you that this has to stop right now."

"Okay," she murmured. She looped her arms around his neck and buried her face in his throat. He smelled of the sea and the sun. Vital and alive. Her tongue discovered his pulse.

"Lily," he groaned, moving his hands to set her away.

"You taste good."

Already, he was wavering. He hadn't wanted her on his boat and here she was a few feet from his bed. They were in each other's arms, and from the way things were progressing, only heaven knew where they'd end up.

"I said, no more." Forcefully Jake moved away from her. Lily's expression fell into a mixture of bewilderment and hurt.

"I told you before, I want to put an end to this nonsense. You women are all alike."

"Jake—"

"It was the same thing with Elaine." It hadn't been, but Lily didn't know that and Jake was desperate to extract himself before things went any further. He had to act fast.

"I'm not anything like Elaine."

"The two of you could be sisters. You think a woman has the right to drive a ring through a man's nose and lead him around."

"That's not true." Lily struggled to swallow back her indignation.

"You women are never satisfied. There's always something that needs to be changed."

"What have I ever asked you to change?"

"My writing. At first you were content to read the short stories, but oh no, those didn't make enough money, so you started pressing me to write novels."

"But I thought…"

"The crazy part of all this is that for a time I even considered it."

Lily took a step back, staring up at Jake. She slowly shook her head, still having trouble believing that this was Jake speaking to her—the man who only minutes ago had kissed her and held her so lovingly in his arms.

"Elaine almost ruined my life and I almost let her. Thank God I saw the light in time."

"Jake…" Recklessly, Lily tried one last time to reason with him.

"You aren't any better than Elaine, worming your way into my life, using me, and then taking it upon yourself to mold me into whatever you want."

"I've never tried to change you."

"Oh that's right. You want to *save* me. Well, listen and listen good. I like my life. I don't want to be saved. Got it?"

"Would you stop shouting long enough for me to say something?" Lily demanded.

"No. Enough's been said."

"It hasn't!" she shouted. "I like you the way you are and I have no intention of saving you."

Jake snorted. "That was what Elaine said."

"I'm not Elaine!" She stabbed a finger in his direction.

"Right," he snickered.

"There's no reasoning with you when you're like this."

"Then it would be best if you left, wouldn't it?"

She didn't say anything for several seconds. "Are you kicking me off your boat?"

"I'm saying—"

"Don't say anything…it's not necessary. I get the picture. I won't bother you again…and I'll never, ever come on board the *Lucky Lady* again. You've made your point perfectly clear." She turned quickly and moved up the steps in a huff.

Jake didn't move. Above him, he heard Lily's footsteps as she hurried across the deck. Her steps were heavy and their echo cut straight into his heart. The frustrations of a lifetime of bitterness suddenly surfaced and he struggled against the urge to ram his fist through the side of the boat. He paced the tiny, enclosed area in an effort to compose himself. It was what he wanted. Lily was gone. He didn't doubt her word; she wouldn't be back. He'd driven her away for good. But Jake couldn't imagine what his life would be like without her. There were better ways of handling this situation. He could apologize, but his pride sneered at the thought. No, he'd bide his time and try to forget how deeply he cared for her. That was the only solution to avoid ruining both their lives.

* * *

By the time Lily slid into her seat at the grand piano at the Wheaton that evening, she was outwardly composed. But the inner battle continued to rage. She didn't know which had hurt the most—Jake comparing her to that horrible Elaine, or when he'd told her to get off his boat. Both had devastated her to the point that she hadn't been able to talk to Gram. Lily placed her hands over the ivory keys and her fingers moved automatically, playing from memory. Lily had learned not to involve her mind in the music. If she did, she'd have been half-crazy by now. Her smile was pasted on her mouth, curving her full lips slightly upward.

The manager strolled past her once and Lily dropped her gaze to her hands. Usually his presence meant she had done something that annoyed him. Lily no longer cared. If he fired her, she'd find another job. The monotony of playing the same songs night after night had robbed her musical gift of the natural spark she'd once possessed. She hardly ever sat at the piano to goof around anymore. And all this for what? The only wealthy man she'd met in a year's time at the hotel was Rex Flanders and that had turned out to be a bust. Even now, Jake's negative reaction to the Texan confused her. He hadn't so much as seen Rex and he'd forced Lily into promising that she wouldn't go out with the middle-aged man.

When Lily had finished the first half of the evening's set of music, she took a break. Henry, the senior bellhop, stopped her halfway across the lobby.

"Miss Lily, there's a message for you." He strolled across the carpet to hand her a beige envelope.

Lily accepted the letter and her heart flip-flopped in her chest. For one insane moment, Lily thought it might be from Jake. After a glance at the slanted strokes of the cursive script, she recognized the handwriting as Rex Flanders's.

The first genuine smile of the evening came.

Hello Lily,
I've been thinking about you lately, and about that old song you hunted down for me. As I promised, I'm back in San Francisco and I'm hoping that you'll allow me to show you my appreciation. I meant what I said about taking you to dinner. I insist. It's the least I can do to thank you.

I'll meet you in the lobby at nine-thirty. Don't disappoint me this time.

Rex

Folding the single sheet over, Lily tucked it inside the envelope. She would join Rex for dinner. Her promise to Jake had been made under duress. Besides, she owed him nothing now. He'd made that clear. He had no reason to care if she saw Rex or any other man, for that matter.

Parked outside the Wheaton, Jake leaned against the side of his cab and crossed his arms, watching the entrance. Lily was due out in another hour. He needed to talk to her so he could explain that he hadn't meant what he'd said. The anger had been a ploy to keep her out of his arms, but he hadn't meant to insult her. The apology burned in his chest. The minute she came through those doors he'd go to her and admit he was wrong. That was the very least he could do. She deserved that and a lot more.

Once he'd made his peace with Lily, Jake decided, they had to have a serious discussion about what was going on between them. They had to stop pretending their kisses didn't mean something, that they were simply friends. For his part, Jake was convinced that a serious relationship between them wouldn't work. Their life goals couldn't be more different. He wasn't going to change. And if Lily wanted a wealthy man, then she ought to look elsewhere. She was putting her schemes in jeopardy by flirting with him.

They were reasonable adults. After they'd talked this craziness out of their systems, they could go back to the way things used to be, and continue as friends. They had to acknowledge those feelings for what they were—infatuation. He was flattered that Lily found him attractive. But they could only be one or the other. They could be great friends or good lovers. Of the two, Jake sought her friendship.

Satisfied with his reasoning, Jake checked his watch again. It wouldn't be long. A crooked grin spread across his face. He felt much better now than he had that afternoon.

Lily nervously smoothed a wrinkle from the skirt of her blue dress. She glanced up to find Rex strolling toward her, his eyes alight with appreciation.

"Lily," he whispered, and collected her hands. "You're as lovely as I remember."

Rex looked even bigger and taller than she had recalled. "Thank you."

"Have you been waiting long?"

"No. Only a minute." Actually, she'd changed her mind twice. Not until she neared the huge glass doors at the Wheaton's entrance had she decided to go back and meet Rex.

"Good." His gaze claimed hers. "It doesn't seem a whole month since I first laid eyes on you."

"Time has a way of slipping past, doesn't it?" Once she'd worried about appearing witty and attractive. Now she didn't care; she could only be herself.

"It sure does." He offered her his elbow in gentlemanly fashion. "I know a quiet little French restaurant where the food is excellent."

"That sounds lovely."

"You do like French food?"

"Oh, yes."

Smiling at her, Rex directed Lily toward the front entrance. Once outside, he stepped forward and raised his hand, calling for a taxi.

Jake was parked in the driveway, chewing on the end of a toothpick, wondering what was taking Lily so long. He had almost made up his mind to go inside and find out. As he straightened, the toothpick slipped from his mouth and fell to the ground. Lily was with that Texan. Jake was incredulous. She'd only mentioned the man a couple of times, but Jake knew instantly that the man she'd told him about was the one escorting her now. She'd promised to stay away from that pot-bellied fool. Promised. He'd been right all along. She wasn't any different from Elaine.

Stupefied, Jake watched as one of his colleagues pulled toward the front. The doorman opened the cab door and Lily climbed in the back with the Texan. Jake was so furious that he slammed his fist against the side of his taxi, momentarily paralyzing his fingers.

Well, fine, Lily could date whomever she liked. She was nothing to him. Nothing.

Inside the cab, Lily tossed a glance over her shoulder, wondering if Jake had been out front. Silently she lambasted herself for even looking. He wouldn't be there, of course, especially after a whole week of avoiding her. After what had happened that afternoon, the Wheaton would be the last place Jake would show.

Feeling agitated, Lily fiddled with her fingers. She regretted having agreed to go with Rex. She'd accepted the date for all the wrong reasons.

Rex must have sensed her uneasiness since he chatted the whole way, his deep voice filling the taxi. When she responded with only a polite word or two, he struck up a conversation with the cabdriver.

Lily wondered if the driver, who was a friend of Jake's, would mention it to him. Fervently she prayed he wouldn't, then doubted that Jake would care either way.

The restaurant, Chez Philippe, was one of the most expensive and highly rated in all of San Francisco. Famous people from all over the world were reputed to have dined there. Lily had often dreamed of sampling the excellent cuisine and catching a glimpse of a celebrity.

After arriving at the restaurant, they were seated by the maître d' and handed huge, odd-shaped menus. Lily noted that the prices weren't listed, so she was left to guess at what this dinner would cost Rex. However, she learned long ago that anyone who needed to ask about the price probably couldn't afford it.

"Do you see anything that looks good to you, little filly?"

Their eyes met over the top of the menu. "What would you suggest?" Rex listed a couple of items and Lily smiled absently. The waiter returned and filled their water glasses with expensive bottled water.

* * *

With each passing minute, Jake's anger grew until he could almost taste his fury with every breath. Slamming the door of his cab, he cursed his lack of decisive action when he'd seen Lily with the rich Texan. She'd promised him she wouldn't go out with Daddy Warbucks and with God as his witness, Jake was going to hold her to her word. As hard as it was on his patience, he waited until the cabbie who drove Lily and the Texan returned to the Wheaton.

"Where'd you take them?" Jake demanded in a tone that caused the other driver to cringe.

"Who?"

"You know who. Lily."

"Oh, yeah. That was her, wasn't it?"

"Where did you take them?" Jake demanded a second time.

The driver cleared his throat. "That fancy French place on Thirty-third."

"Chez Philippe's?"

"That's the one."

Jake breathed a quick word of thanks then rushed back to his cab, revving the engine with such force that a billow of black smoke shot from the tailpipe.

Jake's cab roared through the streets toward Chez Philippe's. He ran two red lights and prayed a cop wouldn't pull him over for speeding.

Once he was within a block of the restaurant, Jake pulled to a dead stop. What was he going to do once he arrived? To rush in and demand that Lily leave with him simply wouldn't work. He'd only end up looking like a jealous idiot. He could picture her now, looking up at him with disdain and quietly asking him to leave. He needed a plan. He parked on the street, not wanting the valet to take his cab. The fact was, Jake wasn't sure the valet *would* take it.

Hands buried deep inside his pants pockets, Jake strolled into the classy place as if he'd been dining there for years. The maître d' stepped forward expectantly.

"May I help you, *monsieur*?"

"A table for one," Jake said confidently.

"*Monsieur*, I regret that we only seat gentlemen wearing a suit and tie."

"You mean I have to have a suit and tie even before I can spend my money?"

"That is correct. I sincerely regret the inconvenience."

Jake scowled. "Do you mind if I sit and wait?" He motioned toward an empty chair.

"Sir, we aren't going to change our dress code this evening."

"That's fine, I'd just like to wait."

The stoic expression altered for the first time as the maître d' arched a skeptical brow. "As you wish."

The rush of whispers from the front of the restaurant caused Lily to glance up from her plate. As she did, her breath caught in her lungs. Jake was standing there, and from the look he tossed at her, he was furious.

Eight

Lily felt the blood drain from her face. Jake was looking at her as though it required every ounce of restraint he'd ever possessed not to march across the room and confront her.

"Doesn't that sound like fun?" Rex was saying.

Lily stared at him blankly. "Yes, it does." She hoped her response was appropriate.

"Good. Good," Rex continued, obviously pleased. "I thought a young filly like you would enjoy an evening on the town."

The first time she'd met Rex, Lily had torn Gram's house apart looking for that crazy song on the chance he'd suggest spending an evening with her. A lavish date with a rich man had been Lily's dream for many years. She was a fool if she was going to allow Jake's foul temper to ruin tonight. She forced her chin up a notch. Jake had made his views of her plain, and she wasn't going to let him wreck her evening.

"Where would you like to start?" She planted her elbows on the white linen tablecloth and rested her chin atop her folded hands, staring at him expectantly.

"There's a small dance floor at the St. Francis."

"That sounds grand," Lily simpered.

"We could have our after-dinner drink there as well, if you like."

"That would be wonderful."

From the corner of her eye, Lily noted that Jake was pacing the small area in front of the maître d's desk. A smile tugged at the edges of her mouth. She certainly hoped he got an eyeful. The memory of the insults he'd hurled at her earlier was enough to encourage Lily. She wasn't much of a flirt but with Rex sitting across from her and Jake just waiting for the opportunity to pounce on her, Lily gave it all she had.

Jake had claimed she was a schemer; she was only proving him right. Once he saw the way she behaved with Rex, he would get the message and leave.

The waiter approached their table with the bill. While Rex dealt with it, Lily took the opportunity to glance in Jake's direction. The shock of seeing him had faded and was being replaced by indignation. Jake had a lot of nerve.

"Are you ready?" Rex asked.

"Yes." Lily's heart constricted as Rex pulled out her chair and she stood.

Her wealthy escort placed a hand on

the small of her back, urging her forward. Lily looked up at him with adoring eyes, ignoring Jake. She held her breath as they approached the front desk, wondering if Jake would cause a scene. Indecision showed in his eyes and she quickly glanced away.

For his part, Jake battled with uncertainty. He'd been a fool to have followed her there. He felt he ought to punch the lights out of that oil-rich Texan and grab Lily while he had the chance. But he couldn't do that. Lily would never forgive him and he already owed her one apology.

The hem of her skirt brushed his leg as she scooted past him and Jake jumped back as though he'd been burned. His eyes demanded that she look at him, but Lily refused. She tucked her hand in the crook of the Texan's elbow and glanced up at him adoringly.

Unsure of what he should do, Jake stood where he was for an entire minute, silently cursing. If he had any sense left, which he was sincerely beginning to doubt, he'd go back to the marina and forget that Lily had broken her promise.

Once outside, Jake's feet felt as though they were weighted with concrete blocks. He gave a companionable salute to the valet as he passed.

Lily and the Texan were in the backseat of another cab, pulling out of the circular driveway and Jake stepped back as they sped away.

As he returned to his taxi he increased his pace. He couldn't ignore the gut feeling that something was wrong with Lily and Rex. The *feeling* had always perplexed him. He hadn't *felt* right about Lily and Rick either, but this time the sensation was far stronger. If anything happened to Lily, he'd never be able to forgive himself. Foolish pride no longer dictated his actions; he was driven by something far stronger: fear.

His hand slapped the side of the taxi and he jumped inside and revved the engine. It only took a minute to locate the other cab driving Lily and Rex. Jake stayed a fair distance behind them, fearing that the other driver would suspect that he was following him.

When they entered the downtown core, Jake relaxed. The other cab was in his territory now and Jake wove in and out of traffic without a problem. The driver dropped Lily and the Texan off at the St. Francis Hotel. Jake couldn't fault the man's taste. He rounded the corner and was lucky enough to locate a parking space.

The doorman opened the tall glass door as Jake approached the hotel entrance. Music from the piano bar filtered into the lobby from the cocktail lounge and he headed toward it. Although his gait was casual, his eyes carefully scanned the darkened area for Lily. When he spotted her sitting at a tiny table in the middle of the room, he heaved a sigh of relief.

As inconspicuously as possible, he took a seat at the far corner of the bar so he could keep an eye on her without being seen.

"Can I help you?" The bartender spoke and Jake swiveled in his seat to face him.

"A beer," he replied. "Any kind. It doesn't matter."

"Right away."

Sitting sideways, Jake propped an elbow against the edge of the bar and centered his attention on Lily. She really was lovely. Jake couldn't blame Rex for being interested. Jake recalled the day he'd taken her out on the *Lucky Lady* and the way she'd sat perched on the bow, laughing. The wind had tossed her hair in every direction, making her resemble a sea nymph, soaking in the early summer sun. Something had happened to him that day—something so significant that he had yet to determine its meaning. From that moment on, Jake concluded, his life had been in a tailspin.

The bartender delivered his beer and Jake absently placed a bill on the counter. Holding the thick glass with one hand, he took a long sip. It felt cool and soothing against his parched throat. He set the glass back on the bar.

Glancing in Lily's direction again, Jake noted that Rex had reached for her hand and held it in his own as he leaned across the small table, talking intimately with her. From this distance Jake couldn't read Lily's reaction.

Without thinking, Jake slid off the bar stool and stood. His fist knotted, but he managed to control his immediate outrage. Another man was touching Lily and although it appeared innocent enough, Jake didn't like it. He didn't like it one bit. Furthermore, he trusted that overweight Texan about as much as he did a rattlesnake.

Several couples were gliding around on a small dance floor on the other side of the lounge and Jake watched as Rex stood and helped Lily to her feet. Jake downed the remainder of his beer when the Texan escorted Lily to join the dancing couples, bringing her into his arms. Holding hands was one thing, but dancing was another. There was nothing more Jake could do, but act. He ate up the distance to the dance floor in three huge strides.

Lily wished she hadn't agreed to come to the bar with Rex. She felt like a fraud.

She had no desire to share a drink and conversation and had even less enthusiasm for dancing. Rex's hands felt warm and clammy against her back and she resisted the subtle pressure of his arms to bring her closer.

They'd already circled around the small dance area once when Lily glanced up and noticed Jake coming toward her with abrupt, angry strides. She knew she should be furious, but her heart responded with a wild leap of pleasure. After her behavior in the restaurant, Lily had been disappointed in herself. Rex was a nice man. He didn't deserve to be used. Jake tapped Rex's shoulder. "I'm cutting in." He didn't ask, but simply announced it.

Rex looked stunned. "Lily?"

"That's fine," she murmured, dropping her gaze. "I...I know him. This is Jake Carson."

Jake took Lily by the waist, pressing her to him as he whirled her away.

"Jake—"

"No, you listen to me. What kind of game are you playing?" He pushed the words through clenched teeth. He was being unreasonable but he didn't care. He wanted answers.

"I'm not playing..."

"You assured me that you wouldn't be seeing Daddy Warbucks."

"That was before."

"Before what?"

"Before you *assured me* that I was a nuisance and asked me to leave your precious boat."

"Consequently your promise doesn't mean anything?"

"No," she cried, then changed her mind. "Yes."

"Dinner was bad enough, but did you have to come here as well? What's the matter? Didn't that fancy restaurant give you ample opportunity to flaunt yourself?"

Lily was too outraged to answer. "Let me go."

"No. I'm taking you home."

"Rex will take me home."

"No way. You promised me you wouldn't be seeing that rich bullfrog, and I'm holding you to your word."

"You can't make me do anything." Lily didn't understand why she was fighting Jake when the very sight of him made her heart race. If only he'd stop behaving like an arrogant fool, she'd tell him that she longed for him to take her home.

"I don't have much taste for making a scene, but I won't back away from one if that's what you want."

"You're acting crazy."

"Perhaps."

"There's no question about it. You're bossy, stubborn and unreasonable."

"Great. Now that you've named my personality traits, we can leave."

"Not without saying something to Rex."

Jake relaxed his hold. "I'll do the talking."

"That's hardly necessary."

He didn't answer as he gripped her hand in his and led the way off the dance floor. The other couples cleared a path for them and Lily wondered how much of their heated conversation had been overheard. Embarrassment brought a flush of color to her cheeks.

Rex stood as they approached the small table.

"I'm taking Lily home," Jake informed the older man.

"Lily, is that what you want?" Rex eyed her seriously. His brows formed into a sharp frown as he waited for her to respond.

"Jake's an old friend," she said, trying to explain.

"I see," Rex said slowly.

"I hope you do," Jake added. His hand continued to grip hers as he headed out of the cocktail lounge, half pulling Lily as he went.

In her heels she had difficulty keeping up with his wide strides and paused momentarily to toss an apologetic look over her shoulder, wanting Rex to know she was sorry for everything.

"Are you happy?" she asked, once they hit the sidewalk.

"Very." He thrust his face toward her. "Don't ever pull that trick on me again."

Recalling all lessons on ladylike behavior Gram had drilled into her over the years, Lily battled to keep her temper. She only partially succeeded. "And don't you *ever* do that to me again."

"Keep your promises and I won't," Jake barked.

They didn't say another word until they were inside the cab, headed home.

The anger was slowly dissolving inside Lily. Everything had changed in the past few weeks and she didn't know if it was for the better. A year ago, she'd started playing piano at the Wheaton with so many expectations. In that time she'd dated two wealthy men and met Jake. Rick and Rex weren't anything like she'd dreamed. Jake was Jake: proud, stubborn, and so very good to her and Gram. She'd ached over the loss of something precious and wonderful—her relationship with Jake—and prayed it wasn't too late to salvage it.

"I thought you didn't care anymore what I did," she murmured, longing to explain why she'd accepted Rex's invitation.

"Believe me, it wasn't by choice." His hands tightened on the steering wheel.

"Then why did you..."

"I couldn't care less who you date," he lied smoothly. "But you'd given your word about that Texan and I was determined to see that you kept it."

"That's why you followed me tonight?" Her voice was little more than a whisper.

"Right."

"I see." She clasped her hands together tightly in her lap. She'd hoped that he'd admit that he cared for her and had been concerned about her welfare. But that was clearly too much to expect in his present frame of mind.

Jake dropped her off in front of Gram's and drove away as soon as she closed the car door. Once inside the house she struggled to maintain her composure.

Gram was asleep and Lily was grateful for that. She would have had trouble recounting the events of this evening. Nothing had gone right, starting with accepting Rex's invitation to dinner.

Knowing that any effort to sleep would be useless, Lily wandered into the kitchen and set the kettle on the burner to boil. When it whistled, she poured the boiling water into a mug before adding a tea bag. A loud knock at the front door surprised her and her heart rocketed to her throat. She didn't have time to react when Jake burst in.

"We need to talk," he announced, coming toward her.

Lily couldn't have moved if her life depended on it.

"Well?" he demanded.

"Would you like a cup of tea?" Lily noticed that his defenses relaxed at the offer.

"Yes."

She busied herself bringing down another cup from the cupboard and adding a tea bag to the steaming water. The action gave her a moment to compose her thoughts. Her head buzzed with all the things she longed to say. As much as she tried, she couldn't keep her gaze off the man who filled the doorway, staring at her.

She gestured toward a chair, indicating that Jake should take a seat. She found it bewildering that only minutes before they had been shouting at each other and now they were behaving like polite strangers.

She set the second steaming mug on the tabletop across from her own and sat facing Jake. She gripped her mug and stared down into the black liquid.

The silence grew heavy and Lily was unsure if she should be the first one to wade into it.

But then they spoke simultaneously.

"Lily—"

"Jake—"

"You first," Jake said and motioned toward her with his hand.

"No...you go first."

"All right." Another lengthy pause followed. "I'm here to apologize."

"For what?"

"Come on, Lily, don't play dumb," He accused.

"I'm not." Her own temper flared. "Are you apologizing for this afternoon or for what happened this evening?"

Jake raked his fingers through his hair. The kitchen suddenly felt small and Jake seemed so large, filling every corner. Despite everything she longed to feel his arms around her again, comforting and gentle.

"I see," Jake said finally. "I guess I do owe you an apology for both." His finger fiddled with the handle of the mug. As yet he hadn't tasted the tea, but then neither had Lily.

"I owe you one myself. I don't know what possessed me to go out with Rex. I shouldn't have. I don't know why I did." Her voice was husky. "That's not exactly true. I went with him because I wanted to get back at you for this afternoon."

"I didn't mean what I said." A telltale muscle twitched along his jaw.

Lily raised her eyes to meet Jake's, unsure that she had understood him correctly.

"Those things I said on the boat were spoken in desperation."

"But why?"

"Come on, Lily, surely you've figured it out by now." He pushed back the chair and stood, taking his tea with him. He marched to the sink and then turned back to her, leaning against the counter as he finally took a sip from his mug.

"You mean because we were kissing again?"

"Bingo."

"But I like kissing you."

"That's the problem, kid."

Lily winced at the use of the childish term. "All right, well, we don't ever have to touch each other again."

It wasn't what Jake wanted, but for his peace of mind and for the sake of a treasured relationship, he had little choice but to agree. "That would be best."

"The kissing was just the result of my own curiosity."

"So you said."

Lily's heart was hammering in her throat. She was forced to admit how much she'd come to enjoy Jake's touch and the thought of them never kissing again filled her with regret. She took a sip of her tea, which had grown lukewarm.

Jake followed suit. There didn't seem to be anything more to say but he wasn't ready to leave, so he searched for an excuse to linger. "You were right about me being unreasonable this evening."

She released a short, audible breath that told of her own remorse. "Going out with Rex and flaunting it in your face like that was childish of me."

"So you knew I was waiting tonight."

"No." Her stare found his. She'd hoped, of course, but she hadn't guessed that he'd be there after their confrontation on the sailboat. "My feelings were hurt and I didn't think you'd care one way or the other if I saw Rex—especially after today—so I agreed to dinner. I regretted it from the minute we left the hotel."

"You seemed to be enjoying your meal." His jaw clenched at the memory of Lily in that fancy French restaurant.

Lily swallowed at the lump of pride that constricted her throat. She'd come this far. "That was an act for your benefit. It's stupid, I know, but at the time it made sense."

A crooked grin lifted one corner of his mouth. "You're lucky that me making a scene in that restaurant *didn't* make sense."

"I guess I am." She returned his smile, wondering if there would ever be a time when his expressive eyes wouldn't affect her.

Jake glanced at his watch. "I suppose I should think about heading home." A few more nights like this one and he'd have trouble paying his bills.

"It is late." Lily couldn't disagree with that, but she didn't want him to leave. She never did.

He took one last swallow of the tea and placed the mug in the sink. "I'm glad we were able to resolve our differences."

"We were both wrong."

"Are you working tomorrow?" He already knew she wasn't, but asking delayed his departure.

"No."

"How about an afternoon on the boat?" It was the least he could do.

Instantly, her dark eyes brightened. Lily loved the *Lucky Lady*, and the thought of spending a carefree afternoon with Jake was an opportunity she couldn't refuse. "You're sure?"

No, he wasn't. Spending the day beside her without being able to touch her would be pure torture for him. But he knew it would make her happy.

"Jake?"

"I invited you, didn't I?"

"Then I'd love to."

"It's a date then. Meet me around noon?"

"I'll be there." She followed him through the living room to the front door. "Jake."

He turned, his brow knit with doubts over the sailing invitation. "Yeah?"

"Thank you for coming back. I wouldn't have been able to sleep if you hadn't."

His body relaxed. "Me neither." With that he was gone.

The following morning Lily was humming as she worked around the kitchen. She had a lemon meringue pie baking in the oven and was assembling some pastrami sandwiches when Gram returned from the garden nursery. The older woman carted in a full tray of potted plants.

At Lily's dubious look, Gram explained, "They were on sale."

Continuing to pack the sandwiches, Lily commented, "But aren't you the one who insists that we don't save money by spending money?"

"Good grief, no."

"Are you sure?" Lily tried unsuccessfully to hide a smile.

"Of course I'm sure. I may be seventy-four, but my mind is still good. I'm the one who says that when the going gets tough, the tough go shopping."

Lily burst out laughing. "I love you, Gram. I don't think I let you know that nearly often enough."

"Sure you do, girl."

Lily hugged her grandmother. Gram might be a bit eccentric, but she had given Lily a good life, taking her in and raising her in a home full of love. "I've got some news for you."

"What?" Gram leafed through the mail, tossing the junk mail without a second glance. The rest she stuffed into an overflowing basket on the kitchen counter.

"I'm giving the Wheaton my two-week notice."

Gram looked doubtful. "Now why would you do that?"

"I don't like it there. This morning I saw a job posting for a music director at a daycare center. I already called and booked an interview."

"And you'd enjoy that?" Gram regarded her skeptically.

"I'm sure I would. You know how much I like children."

"That you do. You're as natural with them as you are with us old folks."

Opening the refrigerator, Lily scouted its contents, taking out two red apples.

"You going somewhere?"

"Jake and I are taking out the *Lucky Lady*."

Gram sank into a kitchen chair and

propped her feet up on the one across from it. "Rick phoned last night. I forgot to tell you."

"What did he want?"

"Just to remind you that he was taking you to dinner tonight."

Lily bit into her bottom lip. "Darn." She'd forgotten about that. "Did he say what time he'd be by?"

"Seven. He didn't seem too happy when I told him you were going out with that fellow from Texas."

Hands on her hips, Lily swiveled around. She'd phoned Gram during her break to explain why she'd be late. "You told him?"

"Had to, girl. He'd mentioned swinging by the hotel to see you."

"Great," Lily grumbled. On second thought it was probably just as well. Rick seemed to want to get too serious too quickly, but Rick was nice and deserved someone who would appreciate him.

"How much do you like this Rick fellow?" Gram wanted to know.

"He's all right."

"Seems to be well off."

"He's got money, if that's what you mean."

"That's what you've been wanting."

The words had a brittle edge to them. Lily opened her mouth to argue that Gram made her sound calculating and shallow, but she found she had no ground. That was exactly the way she'd been in the past. Her ambition to marry rich had made her so narrow-minded that it was little wonder she'd been disappointed with both Rick and Rex.

"I'm not so sure anymore," Lily murmured, tucking the lunch supplies into the bottom of a wicker basket. "I've been doing some thinking lately and I feel that there are certain things in life more valuable than a fat bank account."

"Oh?" Gram gave her a look of mock surprise.

"Money's nice, but it isn't everything."

"The next time house taxes are due I'll tell that to the county clerk."

"We've always managed in the past; we'll do so again."

Gram mumbled something under her breath, but she was smiling and Lily wondered what her game was.

"So you're going to spend the day with Jake? I take it you two have resolved your differences?"

"We're working on it," Lily hedged. They'd taken one step forward, but at the moment it seemed a small one. There was so much she wanted to share with Jake and feared she couldn't. Her job at the Wheaton was coming to an end, but she wouldn't tell Jake until she had another one to replace it. Otherwise he might worry. He cared for Gram and her. Lily only wished he cared a little bit more.

Nine

Jake placed the jib sail on the bow of the *Lucky Lady*. He was nervous about this excursion with Lily and regretted having suggested it. However, he realized that Lily loved being on the water and that the invitation to sail would go a long way toward repairing their friendship.

Strolling down the long dock that led to Jake's boat, Lily saw him working on the bow. She paused to admire him. Her heart fluttered at the sight of his lean, brawny figure. He was all man, rugged and so completely different from Rick that it was difficult to picture them as friends. Jake possessed an indomitable spirit and a fierce pride. Of the two men, Rick was the more urbane and sophisticated, but there was a purity of character in Jake. He was true to himself and his beliefs. Rick was too easily influenced by those around him. He considered it important to flow with the tide. Jake was the type of man who *moved* the tide.

"Morning," she called, standing on the pier and waving at him.

"Good morning." Jake straightened and Lily noted he wasn't smiling. Wasn't he pleased to be sailing today? Was he only doing this for her? Hoping to turn things around, she held up the picnic basket enthusiastically. "I packed us a lunch."

"Good thinking." He climbed down from the bow. "Are you ready to cast off?"

"Aye, aye, captain." She saluted and

handed him the basket before climbing aboard. While he fiddled with the ropes, Lily took off her light summer jacket. She'd worn jeans and a sleeveless top, hoping to catch a bit of a tan on her arms. She didn't hold out much hope for this day, but desperately yearned to smooth over the rough edges of their relationship. Jake had been such a good friend. There were things in her life that only Jake knew. She could tell him anything without fear of being criticized or harshly judged. Anyone else would have called her hard-hearted and callous to set her sights on a wealthy man. Not Jake. He'd even gone so far as to introduce her to Rick and try to help her fulfill her ambitions. And she had helped him. Jake longed to be a successful author. He could do it, too. The *New Yorker* wouldn't buy a short story from someone without talent.

"We're going to have nice weather," Jake said, looking to the blue sky.

"Yes, we are." They were tiptoeing around each other, Lily realized, each afraid of the other's response. "Can I raise the sails again?"

"If you want." He kept his sights straight ahead, manning the helm.

Feeling self-conscious and a little unsteady on her feet, Lily climbed to the bow and prepared to raise the sails. She waited until they were clear of the waterway that led from the marina to the deep, greenish waters of San Francisco Bay before hoisting the sails and tying them off. The boat instantly keeled and sliced through the rolling waves.

Holding on to the mast, Lily threw back her head and raised her closed eyes to the warm rays of the summer sun. A sense of exhilaration filled her. Her unbound hair blew behind her head like a flag waving in the breeze. She loved this. Her skin tingled with the force of the wind and the spray of saltwater. "This is great," she called down to Jake a moment later. Finding a comfortable spot, she sat and wrapped her arms around her bent knees. She felt marvelous—better than she had in weeks; giddy with happiness. She looked at Jake and their eyes met. Lily's cheeks grew warm as he studied her. His eyes became serious and seemed to linger on her mouth. She smiled at him. He responded with a short, almost involuntary, grin.

Jake found himself incapable of looking away. Lily was so lovely that the picture of her at this moment, her dark hair wind-tossed and free, would be forever seared in his mind. He yearned to go to her, kneel at her feet, and promise her the world.

He felt as though he'd been punched

in the gut. The emotion he felt for her went far beyond friendship. He was in love. All this time he'd *been* in love with her and hadn't been able to admit it— not even to himself. A frown drove deep grooves in his brow. What was he supposed to do now? He'd always cared for her. Recognizing his feelings couldn't make a difference. There were things that Lily wanted that he could never give her. Fancy parties, diamonds and expensive clothes. From the pittance he earned driving a taxi and writing stories, it was unlikely that he could ever afford those things. He might love her, but he wouldn't let that love destroy her dreams.

Lily studied Jake and noted that he was brooding. She couldn't recall a time when he'd been more withdrawn.

Concerned, she cupped her hands

around her mouth and called out: "Are you hungry?"

Jake stared out across the water before answering. "I could eat something." Actually, he was ravenous but he wasn't sure he was ready for Lily to join him on deck. Now that he'd acknowledged his feelings, it would be ten times more difficult to keep her out of his arms.

Lily hadn't eaten since early morning. "I'm starving." Watching her step, she worked her way toward the opposite end of the sailboat to join him.

Jake watched her as she approached. The sun glittered through her hair, giving it an almost heavenly shine. Her lips were pink and so inviting that the muscles in his abdomen tightened. Each step she took emphasized the lovely lines of her neck and shoulders and the curve of her breasts…Jake's thoughts came to an abrupt halt.

This type of thinking wouldn't do either of them any good. He could fantasize until doomsday about making love to Lily and it wouldn't change anything. She was going to marry some rich man and Jake was going to let her.

Lily glanced up from the picnic basket to find Jake watching her, clearly amused. "Is something funny?"

"No." His gaze shot past her to the water, but when he turned back to her, he smiled, his face relaxing and his eyes growing gentle and warm.

Lily experienced the effects of being near Jake almost immediately. She was so tempted to just reach out and touch him. She sat as far away as she dared without being obvious. Yet she was drawn to him like a homing pigeon to its place of rest.

"What did you pack?" Jake asked.

"Pastrami sandwiches and homemade

lemon meringue pie." She removed the cellophane and handed him a sandwich.

"Mustard?" He cocked one dark brow with the question.

"Your wish is my command."

"Your memory impresses me."

I'm glad something does, she mumbled to herself, suddenly feeling gloomy. She didn't dare get close to Jake, even in the most innocent way. Lily was tired, having slept only a few hours the previous night. She yearned to curl up in his arms and nestle her head against his chest. She looked away, fearing he would take one look at her and know what she was thinking.

"Aren't you going to eat something?" Jake asked. "I thought you said you were hungry."

"I am," she answered, somewhat defensively. Reaching inside the basket, she withdrew another sandwich, unwrapped it and took a bite. "There's cold beer if you want one," she told him.

"Sure." Lily grabbed one for him and another for herself.

"I didn't know you liked beer. I thought you preferred wine."

"I do sometimes. Beer's good too. It's an acquired taste. Gram says it's good for what ails you."

Jake downed a large swallow and wiped his mouth off with the back of his hand. "Gram's right."

Lily took a more delicate swig. The liquid felt cold all the way to her stomach. She took another bite of the sandwich. "My dad was a big beer drinker."

"You've never spoken much of your father."

"He died when I was young." Lily looked at the sails as they billowed in the wind, avoiding eye contact with Jake.

"What about your mother?"

"I don't remember her," she said, her voice growing soft. "The pictures Gram gave me of her make me wish I had. She was really beautiful. But she died of complications following surgery."

"You must have been very young."

"Three. Gram took me in then because Dad traveled so much. I don't think Dad ever recovered from losing my mother. Gram says they loved each other like no two people she'd ever known, except her and Paddy. Yet my parents were nothing alike. Mom was delicate. From her pictures, she looks like a fragile princess. And Dad was this big hulk of guy—a lumberjack sort of fellow. I have wonderful memories of him. Whenever he'd come home it was like Christmas; he brought Gram and me the most marvelous gifts. I saved every one. Mom and Dad's picture sits on my dresser. I'll show it to you sometime if you'd like."

The smile in Jake's eyes widened and spread to his mouth. "You must resemble her."

"Me?" Lily laughed. "No, I'm more like my dad. I've got this big nose and fat cheeks and ears that tend to stick out."

"You're lovely."

"Why, Jake, what a nice thing to say." She laughed and took another swallow of the beer. "When was the last time you had your eyes examined?" It felt good to tease him again. "What about your parents?"

"There's not much to tell. They're both still alive. I don't see them often. I'm kind of the black sheep of the family. My two brothers are successful. One's a bank executive and the other's a physician."

"And you're the almost famous writer." Lily was obliged to defend him. This past month when Lily had been seeing

Rick and Rex had taught her how unfair it was to judge people by their bank balance.

"No, I'm a cabdriver and a failure. After all, they paid for four years of college for me that have completely gone to waste."

"It hasn't been wasted."

"In their eyes it has."

"You're a strong and solid man and if your parents don't see that, then I pity them." Jake was earthy and intelligent. A man of character and grit. He may have chosen a different path than his brothers, but that didn't make him any less a success.

"My mother would like you." His voice was oddly gruff. "She'd see you as just the type who could reform me."

"But you don't want to be saved. Remember?"

"You're right about that." But if anyone could ever do it, it would be Lily. A house, family and responsibilities wouldn't be half bad if he shared his life with her. The change wouldn't come easy, but he would be more prone to consider it with her.

They finished their beer and sandwiches and Jake ate a thick slice of pie, praising her efforts.

The sun shone brightly against the horizon and the boat plowed smoothly ahead through the choppy waters. Gradually, Lily's head began to droop. The beer had added to her sleepiness, and now she fought to keep her eyes open.

Intent on his duties, Jake didn't seem to notice until Lily started to slouch against his side. Instinctively he reached for her, looping an arm around her shoulders and pressing her weight to his side. The sheer pleasure of holding her was overwhelming. And yet it felt so natural. Pressing his face into her hair, he breathed in the fresh scent of her. She reminded him of summer wine.

Closing his eyes, Jake took in another deep breath and held it. He'd never told another living soul about his parents' disappointment in him. His love for Lily surged at the way she'd wanted to defend him. Her eyes had sparked with fiery indignation. A lazy smile spread over his features. The wind changed directions and he expertly manipulated the canvas sails around to catch the power of the moving air.

Relaxed now, he stretched out his legs and crossed them at the ankles. A man could get accustomed to this. The woman he loved was in his arms and the sea was at his command.

Lily stirred, feeling secure and warm. Slowly she opened her eyes and realized the cause of this incredible relaxed sensation. Suspecting that any sudden movement would destroy the moment, Lily gradually raised her face to Jake. His serious eyes met hers.

The sails flapped in the breeze and still Jake didn't move. Lily remained motionless and the moment stretched out until she lost all concept of time. It could have been seconds or even minutes, she didn't know. Jake's face was so close to hers that she could see every line etched in his face. Jake smiled. Then, a fraction of an inch at a time, his mouth edged toward hers.

Lily closed her eyes, surrendering to him. Ever so gradually, his mouth eased onto hers. Lily felt her heart melt, but resisted the urge to lock her arms around his neck. Although she yearned for more, she was unwilling to invite it. Only the day before, Jake had ardently claimed he hadn't wanted this. Yet here he was, holding her, kissing her and looking as though it would take all the forces of heaven and hell to drive them apart.

The kiss lindered for what seemed like a lifetime. When he finally dragged his mouth from hers, Lily didn't protest. Her response had to be careful. It would be tragic to destroy this moment. She kept her eyes closed and savored the feel of his breath as it continued to fan her lips. She could tell that Jake was as affected by the kiss as she.

"Oh, Lily," he whispered. Jake bent his index finger and gently pressed it to her lips. "Did you enjoy your nap?"

Her response was a faint nod.

"Good."

Unhurriedly, as if moving in slow motion, Jake lifted his arm from her shoulders. Lily shifted her weight and stretched. Sitting up straight, she smoothed her hands over her jean-clad thighs, searching for something to say.

"We're doing it again and we said we wouldn't," Jake said.

Lily cast her gaze to the deck. "You're right."

"We should think about heading back. It's been a full afternoon."

Lily felt hurt and cheated. Why did Jake find it so objectionable to kiss her? Every time he did, it was wonderful. "Okay," she mumbled. "If that's what you want."

"Don't you?"

"No. Yes. I don't know anymore. What's wrong with kissing me?" she asked him bluntly.

"Plenty. I'm not right for you." His brow narrowed into a heavy frown. "I'd never make you happy."

"I'm happy with you now," she cried, her voice breaking.

"Sure you are, but it won't last, Lily. I'm saving us both a lot of heartache, understand?"

"No, I don't."

His mouth hardened and he stared straight ahead, effectively closing her out. Lily had seen that look often enough to realize that she might as well argue with a brick wall, for all the good it would do her.

A sudden chill went all the way to her bones. She reached for her jacket. Jake was freezing her out again; but somehow it hurt more this time.

As they neared the marina, Jake momentarily gave her the helm and moved forward to lower the sails. The lump in the back of her throat had grown so large she could barely swallow. Even breathing was difficult. Today should have been special. And now it was ruined.

"Lily, listen. I'm doing this for your own good."

"Stop it, Jake," she all but shouted. "Why can't you be honest, for once? I don't know what you're trying to prove. I couldn't even begin to guess. I'm tired of playing your games."

The *Lucky Lady* glided smoothly into her berth. Lily waited just long enough for the boat to steady before leaping onto the dock.

"Lily, wait." Jake jumped after her, pausing to secure the vessel. "Don't leave like this. We need to talk this out." He didn't know what he could say, but seeing Lily this upset was more than he could bear. He had to find some way to reason with her.

She turned to face him squarely. "Sorry, no time. I've got a date with Rick."

The words hit Jake with all the force

of a freight train. She had a date? Jake held her gaze and a muscle flexed convulsively in his jaw. Apparently it didn't bother her to go from one man's arms to another's. "Then what's keeping you?"

"You certainly wouldn't be interested in keeping me, would you?" Maybe it was cruel of her but she wanted him to experience just a little of what she was feeling. "Rick likes me. He isn't hot and cold."

Sadly she shook her head. "Goodbye, Jake." She turned and walked up the narrow dock. Every step took her farther from Jake and somehow Lily felt she'd never be coming back.

Jake watched her go, his fist knotted at his side. Half of him demanded that he race after her, but the other commanded that he stay exactly where he was. Against all good sense, he'd done it again. He'd kissed her and regretted it, punishing Lily for his own weakness. It wasn't Lily's fault he couldn't control himself around her. Nor was it her problem that he'd fallen in love with her. But something had to be done. And quickly.

In the past, he'd toyed with the idea of packing up and moving down the coast. They couldn't continue on this way. They were confusing one another, fighting their feelings, denying what they yearned for most. He had to get out of her life completely. There was no help for it. He had to leave.

Jumping back on the deck of his boat, Jake moved with determined strides. Now that he'd made up his mind, he felt better.

Belowdecks, he reached for the sea maps, charting his course down the California coast. He was a free man, no ties, no bonds. He could go without a backward glance. Except...

Jake paused. *Except.*

He slumped against the counter. He couldn't leave Lily. It would be like leaving a part of himself behind. Who was he trying to fool? He loved her. Loved her enough to give up the precious freedom he'd struggled to maintain all these years.

He'd sell the boat before he'd lose Lily. The thought nearly paralyzed him. He'd meant it. Lily was worth ten thousand *Lucky Lady*'s.

When a man felt that strongly for a woman there was only one option: marriage. He waited for the natural aversion to overtake him. It didn't. The startling fact was that it actually sounded quite appealing.

His mind conjured up a house with a white picket fence around it. He could see Lily in the front yard planting flowers, pregnant.

That, too, had a nice feel to it. Jake

hadn't thought of it much, but he'd like to have a son. And a daughter would be a joy if she looked anything like Lily.

Marriage, a family, responsibilities, a regular job—those were all the things he'd despised over the years. Jake had claimed they weren't for him. But they would be if he had Lily at his side. All this time he'd had the gut feeling that Rex and Rick were wrong for her. Of course they were. *He* was the one meant for Lily. In time, Jake would give her the fancy things she wanted. He even looked forward to doing it.

Shuffling through his closet, Jake took out his best clothes. He'd shower and shave first so he'd look halfway decent. A man didn't ask a woman to be his wife every day of the week.

"Hi, Gram." Lily walked in the front door and tried to put on a happy face.

Rocking in her chair, Gram glanced away from the TV show she was watching. "You've been crying."

"It...just looks that way. I've got something in my eye."

"Like tears," Gram scoffed, slowly getting to her feet. "What happened?"

"Nothing." Lily's could feel her control slipping. "Jake kissed...me," she finally said.

"Why, that's no reason to cry, child." Gram gave her a perplexed look as if she couldn't comprehend why Lily would find Jake's kiss so repulsive.

"I—I...know...but...he...doesn't... want...me."

"He'd hardly be kissing you if it wasn't what he wanted."

"You don't understand." She wiped the tears from her face. "I'm so in love with him, Gram. But you know Jake. He doesn't want a woman in his life. Loving him has ruined everything. We've lost him."

Gram's look was thoughtful as she slipped her arm around Lily's waist and hugged her close. "Dry those tears. You and I have weathered worse over the years. And as for losing Jake, we can't lose something we never had. Let Jake sort this out for himself. He's a smart man."

"I don't ever want to see him again."

The older woman smiled. "You don't mean that. But I know how you feel. Paddy and me had some pretty good fights in our time."

"We didn't fight," Lily insisted. In some ways she wished they had. An argument would have cleared the air. It might even have brought out the truth and helped them find a solution—if there was one.

Slowly Gram walked into the kitchen

and put on the kettle. "I'll make you a cup of Marmite."

"Thanks, Gram," she said solemnly. She'd spent so much time trying to find herself a wealthy man that she'd allowed herself to be blind to the treasures she already possessed.

The last thing Lily felt like doing was getting ready for her date with Rick. She had to end things. She'd been using him and that couldn't continue.

The doorbell chimed just when Lily was touching up her makeup. The telltale redness around her eyes had faded and she looked reasonably attractive.

Lily stuck her head around the corner to be sure that Gram had answered the door. With the television blaring, Gram often didn't hear the bell. It had gotten so bad that Jake had become accustomed to knocking once and letting himself in. At the thought of Jake, a tiny shudder went all the way through her.

Rick stood awkwardly in the living room and Lily offered him her brightest smile. She wasn't looking forward to this evening. "I'll be with you in a minute."

"Take your time," he said, smiling back at her.

Tonight wouldn't be easy, but she wasn't going to be maudlin.

After grabbing her purse and a light wrap, she rejoined Gram and Rick in the living room, forcing herself to smile.

Knowing Lily would be out with Rick, Jake waited for what he considered a reasonable amount of time before heading over to Gram's. Content now that he'd made his decision, he climbed inside his faithful taxi and absently ran his hand along the empty seat. He'd sell the cab. That would be the first thing to go.

While waiting, he'd scanned the newspaper. Finding a decent job shouldn't be too difficult. Engineers seemed to be in demand, and although his degree had several years' dust on it, he'd been a good student. An employer would recognize that soon enough.

On impulse, Jake stopped at a corner market and picked up a small bouquet of flowers. He didn't know what kind they were; flowers were Lily and Gram's department. Humming, he eased to a stop in front of Gram's house, climbed out of the car and slapped his hand across the hood as he ventured past. He felt good. Once everything was straightened out with Lily, he'd be on cloud nine.

Gram answered his knock and he proudly shoved the flowers in her direction. "Is Lily home yet?"

"Are these for me or her?"

"Both."

"I'd say you're a bit late."

It wasn't like Gram to snap or grumble. Jake glanced at his watch. "It's barely ten."

"That's not the late I'm talking about."

"Is Lily home or not?" His own patience was running short.

"Not. I don't know what's come over you, but Lily came home from her time with you in tears."

Shifting his weight from one foot to the other, Jake cleared his throat. He hadn't expected the third degree from Gram. "I came to apologize for that."

"And I'm telling you, you're too late."

A sudden chill went all the way through Jake. "What do you mean?"

"Rick was here earlier."

"I know." All evening he'd been haunted by the image of Rick kissing Lily. He'd considered intercepting their date, but he'd done that before and had promised himself he wouldn't again.

"Only this time Rick didn't come alone."

Confused, Jake shook his head, not understanding Lily's grandmother. "How do you mean?"

"Rick came a-courting with a two-karat diamond ring in his pocket," Gram explained. "He's requested my permission to ask for Lily's hand."

Ten

"I see," Jake said slowly. The words went sour on his tongue. He did indeed understand. Lily had finally achieved her goal. She'd landed herself a wealthy man. Swallowing back the angry denial that trembled at the end of his tongue, Jake buried his hands deep inside his pants pockets. "I imagine Lily was thrilled?" He raised expectant eyes to Gram. The happy, carefree feeling that had been with him from the moment he'd decided to ask Lily to marry him slowly shriveled up and died.

"I can't rightly say. Rick planned on asking her at dinner this evening."

"Lily will accept." She'd be a fool not to, Jake knew.

"It's the best offer she's likely to get," Gram asserted, eyeing Jake in his best clothes. "But I'll tell her you were by."

"Don't." The lone word burst forcefully from his lips. "It wasn't anything important." He took a step back and bumped into the front door. Abruptly he turned around and gripped the doorknob, needing a moment to gather his thoughts. "Actually," he said, turning back to Gram. "On second thought you can mention that I was here. Tell Lily that I wish her and Rick every happiness."

"Do you want me to tell her anything else?" Gram encouraged with her usual astuteness. "You didn't bring these flowers for an old woman."

Jake's gaze fell on the elephant tusks mounted on the wall and the zebra-skin rug spread in front of the fireplace. Herbie, the shrunken head who Gram claimed was their spiritual protector, sat on the end table in its place of honor. Jake would miss all of it, and Gram with her African chants and wise old eyes.

"No," he murmured sadly. There was nothing left to say. Lily's dreams had come true, and his nightmares were of his own making.

The following morning, Lily sat down at the kitchen table with a mug of hot coffee. She needed the caffeine. The evening with Rick had been a disaster from the start. After he'd learned that she'd gone out with Rex, Rick had panicked and come to her with a huge diamond ring and a marriage proposal. She didn't want to hurt him, but she couldn't marry him either.

The morning paper was spread across the table and Lily mindlessly read the headlines. Gram pulled out a chair to join her. "Where'd the flowers come from?" Lily asked, noting the colorful bouquet in the middle of the table.

Gram glanced up from the comic-strip section of the newspaper and grinned. "A secret admirer."

"Oh?" Gram had attracted more than one man. But to the best of her knowledge, Lily had never known her grandmother to see or talk of anyone except her beloved Paddy.

"Only my secret admirer couldn't decide if the gift was meant for me or you. He finally decided on me."

"And who could this indecisive fellow be? Tom the butcher? Or that new man who's been eyeing you at bingo?"

"Nope. It was Jake."

"Jake!" Lily did her utmost to disguise the wild happiness that shot through her. "Jake was here? When?"

Idly, Gram folded the newspaper to the crossword section and scrunched up her brow as she studied the fine print. "Late last night. It must have been close to ten."

Nearly too overwhelmed to speak, Lily stumbled over her words. "Why didn't you... What did he... Flowers?" She clenched the soft bathrobe at her throat. Jake. Here. Why, oh why, hadn't Gram said anything sooner?

"I don't know what he wanted. He was acting oddly."

Lily jumped to her feet. "I'm going to get dressed. Did he stay long?"

"Five minutes or so. Not long." Gram didn't look up as her pencil worked furiously across the newspaper, filling in the words. "Just remember what I told you the first time we met Jake: you and he were meant for each other."

There was a gleam in Gram's eye that hinted at something more, something she wasn't saying.

"Since Jake came by here, it would only be polite to return the visit. Right?" She didn't wait for Gram to answer her. "He obviously had something on his mind or he wouldn't have come. I mean, it isn't like Jake to stop by unexpectedly." He did exactly that three or four times a week but Lily was grateful her grandmother didn't point it out.

Hardly caring what she wore, Lily dug through her drawer and found a pair of white linen pants and a floral print top. A quick run of the brush through her hair left it looking shimmering and healthy.

At the marina, the first thing Lily noticed was Jake's taxi with a For Sale sign propped against the dashboard. Lily stared at it with disbelief. The money from the short story sale to the *New Yorker* had been good, but not enough to live on. Jake would never sell his source of income.

Hurrying now, she half-ran down the wooden dock that led to his slip. She spotted him immediately, working on the deck, coiling a large section of rope around his arm. Her pace slowed. Now that she was here, there didn't seem to be anything particular to say. Although he was facing her, he didn't acknowledge her approach or give any indication that he'd seen her.

"Morning, Jake." She stood with her hands clenched together in front of her.

He ignored her, continuing to wind the thick rope around his arm, using his elbow as a guide.

"There's a For Sale sign on the cab."

"I know."

"But why?"

"It's for sale." His voice held no welcome.

Lily could see that this topic wasn't going anywhere. "Gram said you were by the house last night."

"I was."

If he didn't stop with that stupid rope and look at her soon, she was going to rip it out of his arms. "The flowers are lovely."

Jake's mouth tightened. "Consider them a goodbye present."

Her heart pounded wildly in her cars. "Goodbye?"

"Yeah, I'm moving down the coast."

"This is all rather sudden, isn't it?"

"I've been thinking about it for some time."

Lily set her hands on her hips. "You'd move just to spite me, wouldn't you?"

For the first time, he halted and glanced up at her, his eyes a brilliant green. His feet were braced slightly apart as if anticipating a fight. "You're not making any sense. I'm moving because…"

"Because you're afraid."

Jake snorted. Inwardly, he admitted that she was probably right. He couldn't be around Lily without wanting her and the best thing for them both was to remove the temptation. "I've fought in Iraq, tangled with drunks who couldn't afford to pay their fare, and listened to your grandmother sing an African chant over my head. I'd say you have little reason to accuse me of cowardice." That, too, was a half-truth. Just being close to Lily caused him to tremble. What had made perfect sense the day before seemed like utter stupidity now. He loved her, yes. But that didn't mean they should get married.

"You're going away because of me."

"Yes!" Jake shouted, feeling angry and unreasonable. "I have this particular quirk about being seen with a married woman."

"I'm not married."

"Not yet, but you will be. Gram told me about Rick's proposal."

She held up her bare left hand, fanning her fingers. "I turned him down."

"That wasn't a smart move."

"I don't love Rick."

"That's your problem, Lily. You've got too much conscience. Loving him isn't necessary. Rick can give you all the fancy things you want."

"He can't give me what I want the very most."

"Give him time."

"Even that won't work," she assured him.

"And what is it that you want so badly?"

"You."

His dark eyes found hers, stunned and staring. "You don't mean that."

"I love you, Jake Carson."

"I don't have the money to buy you a fat diamond."

"A simple gold band will do." For every argument Jake presented, she would find a solution. She hadn't come this far to let him slip away.

"My home is right here. There isn't going to be any fancy house." *Except maybe one with a white picket fence and a row of flowers at the front.*

"In case you hadn't noticed, I love the *Lucky Lady.* We'll live right here."

"And what about kids? There's no room for children here." He gestured casually at the confines of the sailboat.

"Then we'll buy a bigger boat."

"I told you before that I can't give you the things Rick could." He didn't know why he continued to argue. He loved her.

"No, you probably can't. But I've learned how meaningless diamonds are. I love you, Jake, and if you love me back, I'd consider myself the wealthiest ex-piano player in town."

Jake's defenses relaxed as he let the rope fall to the deck. He held out a hand to Lily, guiding her safely aboard the *Lucky Lady*'s and into his arms. He buried his face in her hair and held her for several minutes, just breathing in the fresh fragrance of her. "I love you so much that part of me would have died to stand by and watch you marry Rick."

"Then why would you have let me?" Even now she couldn't understand his reasoning.

"Because I wanted to give you all those material things you deserved. But in order to do that, I had to let you go."

Lovingly, Lily cupped his face. His

strong, proud features seemed to intensify with each word.

Lily sighed as relief washed over her. "The only thing I'll ever want is you."

"I'm already yours. I have been since that night in the attic and probably long before then, only I refused to acknowledge it." His strong arms held her closer as if he feared she would escape him.

Lily's eyes gleamed with happiness. "Gram was right."

"About what?"

"Before I left this morning, she told me that you and I were destined to be together."

Unable to resist any longer, Jake tenderly kissed the corner of her mouth. "How could she be so sure of that?"

Lily's hands toyed with the hair at the back of his neck. "Remember the day we met in front of the Wheaton when Gram chanted over you?"

His mouth found her cheek. "I'm not likely to forget it."

"Gram was sealing our fate. That was a fertility rite. We're doomed to live a long, happy life. And from what Gram said, we're going to need a very large boat in the years to come."

Jake chuckled. "I can live with that," he told her, and then he kissed her, certain that this time he'd never let go.

* * * * *

The
ESSENTIAL COLLECTION

YES! Please send me the *Essential Collection by Debbie Macomber* in Larger Print. This collection begins with 3 FREE books and 2 FREE gifts in the first shipment, and more free gifts will follow! My books will arrive in 8 monthly shipments until I have the entire 51-book *Essential Collection by Debbie Macomber.* I will receive 2 or 3 FREE books in each shipment and I will pay just $4.99 U.S./$5.89 CDN. for each of the other 4 books in each shipment, plus $2.99 for shipping and handling. *If I decide to keep the entire collection, I'll have paid for only 32 books because 19 books are FREE! I understand that by accepting the 3 free books and gifts places me under no obligation to buy anything. I can always return a shipment and cancel at any time. My free books and gifts are mine to keep no matter what I decide.

261 HCN 1446   461 HCN 1446

Name _____ (PLEASE PRINT)

Address _____ Apt. #

City _____ State/Prov. _____ Zip/Postal Code

Signature (if under 18, a parent or guardian must sign)

Mail to the **Harlequin® Reader Service:**
IN U.S.A.: P.O. Box 1867, Buffalo, NY 14240-1867
IN CANADA: P.O. Box 609, Fort Erie, Ontario L2A 5X3

* Terms and prices subject to change without notice. Prices do not include applicable taxes. Sales tax applicable in N.Y. Canadian residents will be charged applicable taxes. This offer is limited to one order per household. All orders subject to approval. Credit or debit balances in a customer's account(s) may be offset by any other outstanding balance owed by or to the customer. Please allow 4 to 6 weeks for delivery. Offer available while quantities last. Offer not available to Quebec residents.